Copyright © Fike Daodu, 2021

All rights reserved.

No part of this book may be reproduced in any form by an electronic or mechanical means, including information storage and retrieval systems, without permission in writing from the publisher, except by a reviewer who may quote brief passages in a review.

This is a work of fiction. Names, characters, places, and incidents either are the product of the author's imagination or are used fictitiously. Any resemblance to actual persons, living or dead, events, or locales is entirely coincidental.

First paperback edition May 2021

Published by Kindle Direct Publishing

table of contents

prologue

i think the world owes me an apology

for every "we don't want you here"

that has punctured through my chest.

for the idea of beauty that has

never included me.

the world owes me an apology

for that child

who called me black

like it was

a dirty word.

rolling off his young tongue like venom.

as if my Blackness will fall off my body like

specks of dust,

falling into the wind

and drifting away into an infinite atmosphere.

the world owes me an apology

for the boys

who walked past me in the halls

and muttered the w o r d

loud enough for my insides to be

torn apart

like loose-leaf paper.

an apology is necessary for

hiding my history,

the multitude of creations,

the star-blessed minds,

the universe-rivaling empires

that went ignored.

the world owes me an apology for

keeping me invisible

just like my predecessors

so that every time i open the stories emanating from my screen

or the

weathery pages of books,

i am invisible

although i e x i s t.

an apology is necessary

for brushing me under the rug,

setting the rug on fire

and turning a blind eye to my presence

when i exist

and when

all i've ever wanted was to be *seen*

but now i burn

and the world sniffs my ashes

while pretending they had never set me on fire

in the first place.

black speck

Okay, so remember that school you used to go to?

You know, that nice one. Modern looking, maybe a smidge traditional. Relatively large, spacious classrooms, nice uniforms and a strict dress code. Yeah, that's the one; pretty Christian, pretty private, pretty *white*. And in all honesty, that last fact in itself isn't the problem.

No, the problem is the fact that you're in this sea of white, and you're the one black speck.

On top of that, the one thing that I'm sure might resonate oh-so-deeply with you is that moment when the teacher would decide to talk about racism or slavery.

And every single eye would be on you.

That's me right now. And when I say "every single eye," I mean *every single* eye: from the kids who could normally give less than a crap about history class, to the other top tier nerds in front who barely interact with me if they can help it.

They're not even subtle about it, and pale eyes are burning into my skin, which is practically on fire, by the way.

Meanwhile, we have Ms. Wilson in front, short, dirty blond hair tucked precariously behind her ear, as she goes on about the Atlantic slave trade, and how my ancestors were whipped and tortured and abused.

Fun.

Her eyes flicker to me for almost a tenth of a second before they go back to blatantly avoiding me.

I hear a sound from behind me, a scoff or snicker of some kind. I'm thinking some strange mix of the two.

My eyes drift in the direction the sound came from as subtly as they can.

Messy hair, a consistently arrogant grin stretched onto his lips, his entire aura dripping in pure *future fratboy.*

Brett. Brett McSomething. McKelly? McClain? I'll never remember.

He's positioned with his eyes on the teacher, a pencil lazily positioned between his thumb and forefinger, and the shadow of a smirk on his lips. Move up a bit and you'll see his pale blue eyes and brushed brown hair that he's certain makes him the most attractive being in the space.

Brett is the one your parents should've warned you about: a never-dropping cold expression, a cool demeanor that commands the universe, a scathing glance that drags all attention to him in seconds. When the universe fears you, you're indomitable.

With Brett, there's no semblance of calm, no thoughtfulness, no understanding of the fact that he *isn't* the sun, or that the rest of us *don't* in fact orbit around him like serf-esque planets.

However, it's far too early and I haven't had any coffee, so I don't dwell on the thought.

Instead, I will my gaze back to the front to Ms. Wilson who is emphatically talking about how everyone was negatively impacted by the slave trade, or how it gave descendents of slaves better opportunities than their African counterparts, or something equally as scary and staggeringly inaccurate.

Even so, I'm planning on saying exactly nothing.

After all, that's my role in the school. The black girl that does not utter a word unless mandatory. Someone who stays quiet through every untruth told during history class; an aid to help the majority feel comfortable.

As a "minority", in this country and in this class, I'm the one student whose ancestors actually lived through the hell that Ms. Wilson is trying so hard to downplay.

Minority. Strange how the word slips from people's lips in such an *othering* way.

As in, *one of those things is not like the other.*

Brett raises a hand as Ms. Wilson is speaking and I internally exhale an exhausted gust of air.

"Yes, Brett?" she asks, dropping whatever she was saying to let him speak.

My mind flickers back to the few times that I've raised my hand in this class, Ms. Wilson's response usually being a "*hold your thought, Amina, I'll get back to you in a minute.*"

She's never actually gotten back to me, but I digress.

"I'm wondering why all this focus on black slavery is necessary," he starts, and other students physically recoil at the dreaded word, and the unapologetic audacity he possesses to ask that bold a question smack in the middle of class, "seeing as tons of other races were enslaved." He finishes it with a glance in my direction as though he's waiting for me to say something.

I say nothing.

"That's a good question, Brett," Ms. Wilson lies through her teeth. Although, maybe she genuinely believes it. I'm not sure which is worse. "It's because as good citizens *and students,* it's important to look back on history and understand the mistakes that have been made in order to improve." She nods emphatically, grey eyes wide and passionate.

My mind tosses that thought over in my mind; whether slavery should be classified as a 'mistake'. After all, the word *'mistake'* is for when you drop a fruit in the grocery aisle. A *mistake* is when someone jostles another person at the airport. A *mistake* is when you forget your math homework at home the day it's due.

Capturing and enslaving an entire race for over four centuries? I trill my lips. Not sure if *mistake* is the word she's looking for.

That being said, I'm sure the answer is supposed to satisfy Brett, but he's not done. "Interesting point, Ms. Wilson," he nods, speaking in the charismatic way he always has, "but I feel like it's become a bit of a crutch for the black community and is starting to do more harm than good."

A blonde girl to my left makes a small gasp at the somewhat alienating label of "the black community" and my eyebrows fly upwards at the word "crutch".

There's *some* value in talking about how you snatched people from their land, shipped them halfway across the world, tortured, abused and assaulted them, hung them, set them on fire, and benefited off their enslavement for centuries. I bring my bottom lip beneath my teeth. History can't be erased. Brett knows this.

Of course, I'm better off *not* voicing that statement.

Ms. Wilson visibly fumbles for words and Brett raises an arrogant eyebrow, waiting for the lady to formulate a coherent sentence. "I don't know if that's particularly appropriate, Brett." Her eyes dart to me, "I think it's still important to talk about since it's quite a significant part of global history and... " she chuckles nervously, "this *is* history class, after all."

Her words are feathers, barely grazing the surface.

There's more to the Triangle Trade that separates it from other types of enslavement.

That's what I want to say.

No other slavery was based on race. That's what I would add. After all, if there's anything I've learned from Debate with Mr. Pham, context in an argument is everything.

I tilt my head to the side.

If I had a voice, I would tell the class that the belief that people were inferior due to their race was what gave slave owners the liberty to do whatever the hell they wanted to their slaves.

Shaking my head, I click my pen. Once, twice.

If I had a voice, I would state that racism was created to justify it. Slavery. What I *should* say to the class is that racism was the game changer; something unseen in other types of slavery.

Also happened to be the first and only large-scale slavery operation that history had ever seen.

Tilting my head to the side, I hold my pen to my bottom lip in thought.

Comparison, analysis. Always emphasized in an argument.

Whoever was the descendant of a *Roman* slave some two thousand years ago? Not exactly distinguishable from a descendant of a Roman emperor in this day and age.

Ergo, they can't be treated differently.

In another world, I would've told Brett that Roman slaves were literate, were allowed to read, had slaves of *their own*. Meanwhile, black slaves were lynched or tied to train tracks for even *attempting* to read.

I exhale a silent laugh. There's a reason that the word 'slavery' is associated with the Atlantic slave trade. My lips quirk upwards. *It was one of a kind.*

However, in this world, I don't utter a word to Brett. *This* world is far too big for me to fit into. In this world, I'm miniscule and silent and non-existent, and my words are not meant to rise to the atmosphere.

"Well, I think—" Brett starts, ready to continue grilling Ms. Wilson, but the bell rings, saving us from the rest of the painfully uncomfortable conversation.

Practically jumping to my feet, I shuffle my supplies, more than ready to be done with *that* conversation, and the other teenagers around me seem just as eager to head out.

Eyes flicker about uncomfortably, eyes that were not-so-subtly burning into my skin moments ago.

“We’ll continue this discussion next class,” Ms. Wilson forces a pretentious smile onto her lips and Brett rolls his eyes once her gaze is off him.

I tuck my stuff into my backpack as Ms. Wilson lets us know about the homework for today, and I’m out the door a few moments later, behind the swarm of kids that are leaving the classroom.

I raise a hand to the side of my face. Still burning hot. Then I’m shaking my head, heading over to my locker and making sure to avoid brushing past anyone.

I’ve always seen history class as a living, walking nightmare. Stu-Co elections are fast arriving and all competition is hashed out in classrooms.

That being said, Brett McWhatever doesn’t necessarily have competition. Not anywhere else, and certainly not in the classroom.

A feathery grin curves onto my lips.

Typical.

cafeteria things

I've always seen the hallways as a warzone.

Essentially, a war zone consisting of manicured teens all decked out in vests, blazers and a kilt or pants.

My primary objective is getting through the hallway alive.

The statement might be a slight exaggeration, but in all honesty, there are a multitude of peers willing to trample me if I give them the opportunity to.

So, I spend all my time dodging past anyone and everyone who comes my way. I clutch my books to my chest, speed walking through the hallway, but making sure to weave past everyone like I usually do.

I mean, it's better than being shoved to the ground, so there's that.

Here's the deal with Elkwood Preparatory Academy; if I'm walking through the hallway and I'm walking directly opposite of someone, there's a 99% chance they're going to shove past me, or wait expectantly for me to get out of *their* way.

And yes, the whole shoving thing gets old really quickly. Especially because after *they* run into me, they push past me, sending me a glare, as if *I* was the one who wasn't looking where I was going before we crashed into each other.

Elkwood teens just have that attitude, you know? Some of them just scrunch up their noses like I'm the most insignificant thing in the world, others just blatantly ignore me, shoving me to the side and not looking back for a second.

What can I say? The handbook guidelines of respect for each and every student have been practiced and executed extremely well.

A sardonic smile slips onto my lips as I dodge one of the girls hurtling down the hallway with her best friends, chatting loudly about what went down last weekend.

I have to shove everything into my locker before heading towards the next warzone: the cafeteria.

I make my way to my locker in one piece, and start to unlatch the lock.

The cafeteria is a warzone that puts everything else to shame. Now, I wouldn't necessarily say it's as life-threatening as the hallways, because those are a whole other type of chaotic.

My locker unlocks, and I shove my backpack and supplies inside, grabbing my card and locking it up again.

However, I *would* say that the cafeteria is a different type of life-threatening. It's the type of life-threatening that messes around with your mind, more so than your physical safety.

I head down the hallways that are almost cleared out by now, swinging the lunch card in my hands. I inhale deeply once I get to the entrance of the cafeteria before letting out a breath and making my way into the chaotic space.

The noise is out of control, but the most disturbing aspect of the entire situation are the eyes that follow your every step.

If it wasn't clear before, I'm not exactly the most popular being at the school. Elkwood sees me as an outsider, so I easily slide into the role of an outcast. The role consists of going to the furthest table in the cafeteria, and sitting alone at said table after grabbing my cafeteria lunch, avoiding any eye contact whatsoever. Safest route to go.

More often than not, it seems like the school has an anti-Amina policy that's something privy to only the students (and some faculty, but I digress). I'm almost one hundred percent sure that the staff isn't as oblivious to the whole issue as they like to appear.

I make my way into the lunch line, hands clasped, feet tapping on the tiled floor beneath me. I think the lunch line is problematic for various reasons.

1. The White Bros™

2. Card Guy
3. The girls and the way they talk to the lunch ladies

Let's start with number 1. The White Bros™ are people you've probably interacted with once in your life. They're essentially the guys that are decent in relation to sports, but not the greatest when it comes to grades. They're future frat boys, and you can tell by the fact that they don't have any self control whatsoever.

Exhibit A: Tyler Thompson. He's ridiculously tall, standing at a solid 5' 11" despite the fact that we're just getting into sophomore year. Right now, he's kicking the shins of his friends who are all loitering nearby, harassing each other and being their usual rowdy selves.

The White Bros™ are also the same guys who let each other cut the line, despite the fact that there are people behind them that want to get lunch just as quickly as they do. In a final word, they're future frat boys, "*all american boys*", and every interaction they have with me tends to drip in condescension and the attitude that no matter what they say, they're inherently right.

Number *2.* Card Guy; the guy who swipes our lunch cards. Not going to lie, he strongly resembles a stoner, what with his black beanie, pale skin, shoulder length red hair, and the abundance of piercings and tattoos covering his lanky, hunched-over body.

In all honesty, Card Guy is fairly creepy and the rumours circling him reflect that notion. His eyes are also always puffed up and slightly bloodshot, and I've never actually seen his eyes without that sinister look to them.

In simple terms, he's somewhat sketchy, and I wouldn't be surprised if he's been arrested before. But only long enough for him to be bailed out and rehired as cashier, staring down students with that *not-fully-here* expression.

Finally, number 3. The girls are visually appealing. Every billboard I pass by seems to support that notion. They're also all similar-looking with slender bodies, tall stances, and heart shaped faces. So, they're imposing in a way, and they use that to their advantage.

See, the lunch ladies are all Marias, Camilas, and Andreas. Ironically, they're absent from teaching staff, despite the fact that Andrea Jiminez would probably be a better science teacher than Candace Jones. Ionic compounds were absolute Greek to me until I showed the worksheet to Andrea as I was passing by. Said lady explained the entire concept in under thirty seconds. Something that Jones wasn't able to do in two weeks. Once Andrea was done, it *clicked.*

I bring my bottom lip beneath my teeth, mind swirling with the thought. She'd make a great science teacher.

Either way, while ordering lunch, the Cassandras, Lindseys and Allisons are more than slightly irritating whenever they interact with the lunch ladies.

They're somewhat condescending, from the way that they barely utter a word to them unless they're saying "more" or "less" to the patronizing smiles they dish out on a daily basis. Now, it's not all of the girls, but it's a good amount of them. It's also extremely uncomfortable for me whenever they grab their trays and walk away without the simple courtesy of a "thank you."

The rest of the girls essentially chat the lunch ladies up, but really, it could also be seen as grilling.

"How's your baby?"

That's sure to go on for a long time, given that they don't mix up who's having a baby, and who isn't.

"I went to Mexico last summer."

Probably one of the most amusing but also awkward conversations. My best guess is that they're trying to forge connections in the way they know how. They chat about their trips for what feels like forever, and most of the conversation consists of the bracelets they got, or complaints about some of the hotel staff in whatever resort they stayed at.

Plus, the conversations tend to take a couple of minutes, and the girls genuinely act like there's no one waiting in line behind them.

I give a smile to one of the lunch ladies as she plops the pizza in my plate, along with a brownie, sending a *thank you* her way. Making my way down the line, I grab my apple juice and whatever else I need before I make it to the end of the line where Card Guy is seated, leaning back in his chair and giving me his usual unamused look.

I give him a tight lipped smile and Card Guy lazily holds out his hand. I pass him my card, and he takes it, swiping it before pressing some keys on his computer.

"Good to go," He drawls, handing my card back to me. His red hair is in dreadlocks today. A recent headline flashes to my mind, one involving a black kid in the neighboring town being suspended for wearing dreadlocks to school. I purse my lips in thought.

Card Guy might be "trash" according to the student body, but he's definitely not going to be getting kicked out of school for wearing dreadlocks anytime soon. My polite smile falters slightly, and I utter a quick *thank you* before making my way to a table towards the back.

I slide into my usual seat, positioned far away from everyone else. I grab a slice of pizza from my plate, holding it up as my eyes scan over the cafeteria.

Elkwood has a distinct cafeteria set up. Is it like every other stereotypical high school you'll see? Not exactly. It varies. For example, towards the center of the cafeteria are the kids who dominate the school, smug and arrogant from their upward-tilted chins to their rolled back shoulders.

Some of them are athletes, some of them are smart kids, or kids who think of themselves as smart. Others are spoilt rich. The requirements? They all have to be at least a solid eight on the attractiveness scale, and they also have to command all attention as soon as they step into a room.

If you haven't guessed, Brett McSomething is a regular at the table.

I, on the other hand, stay as far away from the table as I can. I'm safer that way. My interactions with those kids are virtually non-existent, but the rare times we *do* interact, it's painfully awkward, and dripping with passive aggression. So, there's that.

Down towards the back left of the cafeteria are the theatre geeks. In another dimension, they might be my crowd. Piercings here and there, blue and purple hair dyes, cackles and faces decorated with vibrant and cool coloured makeup that is definitely against the dress code.

In the table across from them sit the Asians and the Gamers. So, disclaimer: there are about six or so Asians in the entire school. South Asian, East Asian, Centra; Asian. The Asian table has some other people thrown in, like this disabled girl, Mia, along with an Arab girl, Yasmine, (still qualifying as Asian) and some of the video game geeks. We don't really talk. If we do have interactions, they're somewhat forced and slightly awkward.

Two tables away, we have the Ambiguous Whites. They're essentially the people with olive skin and dark hair. Some might be part Greek or Italian, others have some other mixed blood down the line. Some claim that they're part Native American or 'Indian' like a good amount of people still say in this town. I honestly can't tell, but they pass as white(ish), so I've always just labelled them as the Ambiguous Whites. Not unlike the Kardashians or some of the more popular YouTubers or TikTokers.

In a few words, they're not the nicest. At least not when they interact with me. Fortunately, most of Elkwood doesn't have the greatest interactions with me, so I can easily smile it off now.

Although, years ago, I let tears stream down my cheeks as my parents murmured condolences and apologies. Time made it easier for me to let everything slide.

Of course, there's the one exception at the dominant table, because a few seats from the center sits the only other black kid in the school.

Emory Richards.

Medium brown skin, dark almond eyes, all topped with a shiny white grin.

Emory, Emory, *Emory.*

In a way, people like him, but they don't *care* about him. The girls' hands always find their way to his hair, the guys always let out a few drug related jokes whenever they feel up to it, despite the fact that most of the guys are the ones getting their hands on vapes and other damaging substances. Emory on the other hand? Completely clean. Not like that stops them, though.

I hate seeing it.

I doubt Emory's a big fan of the comments or the unwanted touching either, but he lets it pass. Sometimes I wonder if he's playing the role of a lapdog, if he genuinely believes that it's okay for him to be treated like this, if he genuinely believes that they like him. However, the scene shifts when I see the occasional winces, when I see

Emory's pretty smile falter, and then I realize that maybe Emory Richards isn't as lighthearted as he likes to portray himself.

Maybe Emory is just playing his cards right.

And it makes me wonder, is it worth it to let that all slide? *Why* does Emory need to play his cards right? Why does Emory need to be the human embodiment of diplomacy?

I push my plate away, slightly, my hands carefully gripping my kilt, my table empty as ever. Emory's gaze meets mine for a tenth of a second from across the cafeteria, and then it hits me:

Emory is trying to avoid being *me.*

He's trying to avoid being the outcast that he could become in mere moments.

And all of a sudden, my appetite dissipates in a second.

to kill self-respect

English class always smells like one of those cheap air fresheners. Maybe a lily one, or something with a tinge of lavender. I can't be certain. Sometimes, English class feels like the only class that gets me. Other times, it feels like a hellhole I can't escape, with a teacher that is just as confusing as the variety of posters in her room.

Ms. Daniels.

On the younger side, definitely. At least, compared to the majority of the other teachers. Where wrinkles and lines have made their homes on other teachers' faces, Ms. Daniels' skin is smoother, less callous, less rough. Her voice is younger, too. Lighter, less raspy.

Now, she's standing in front of the class, organizing the plan for today, dark hair falling down her back and floral skirt billowing with her movements.

I can't say she's entirely mean. Not like Mr. Miller from I.T. or Ms. Moore, the vice principal whose glare cuts into me every time we cross paths.

However, Ms. Daniels is almost distant.

She skirts around some student interactions. Her cat eyes zero in on some students, gloss over others. She's a lot more left-leaning than the other teachers at school. Is that a good thing? Not necessarily. She's one of those liberals that are constantly: *help the poor African children* or *segregation was sad, but it was a long time ago* or *your English is* so *good.*

She's one of those people who you can tell in an instant has never interacted with a black person. As in had a full fledged, double-sided, *let's talk* type of conversation with a black person. I guess she tries to sympathize but she hasn't ever really empathized.

"Last year," Ms. Daniels starts, making her way to the front of the classroom, "we all went over Harper Lee's *To Kill A Mockingbird* as a class. For sophomore year, the intent is to revisit this book in a mature, well-rounded discussion."

Some murmurs fill the class, and Ms. Daniels clicks her ball point pen before continuing, "I expect you to take notes, have a *respectful* discussion with your peers," She eyes some of the students towards the back who chuckle, "*And* to listen and wait before speaking, *Ryan,*" The redhead's eyes flicker away from his lap, (or really, his phone), before his eyes flicker up to hers, eliciting laughter from the class as he gives her an exaggerated thumbs up.

Ms. Daniels shakes her head before continuing, "We're revisiting To Kill A Mockingbird to gain a stronger understanding of the text now that you're all older, and *hopefully,* more mature." Light laughter. "We'll also compare and contrast said book to our next novel that I'll be revealing later on this month."

She places her hands on her hips as the students stare back at her. "We're setting our debate up here," She vaguely gestures around where she's standing, "So, pull your seats around the front area, and we'll begin shortly."

A few grunts and murmurs follow her instructions, and soon, the shuffling movements of chairs and the clinking sound of people bumping into each other fill the classroom.

Before I can blink twice, we're situated in a circle, people talking amongst themselves. Ms. Daniels turns on the smartboard. "Listen up," She says, and the class quiets, albeit slowly, "I have the guiding questions up here on the SmartBoard. They'll lead our discussion for today."

So, the discussion starts. I'm almost thankful that Brett isn't in this class, but I sink further into my seat when I realize some of his lackeys are present.

The discussion starts with the way The Great Depression influenced the plot, the characterization of characters and the seemingly different stories focusing on Boo Radley and the court case surrounding Tom Robinson. Then the conversation moves over to the symbolism of the mockingbird.

"The mockingbird represents innocence." I find myself saying after Ms. Daniels gives me a pointed look. "Moreover, the title: *To Kill A Mockingbird* is essentially describing: to kill someone's innocence." Ms. Daniels keeps her eyes on me, silently urging me to continue, and the rest of the students keep their eyes on me, as I let out a breath before continuing. "This story specifically revolves around Scout finally opening her eyes to the injustice and racism that exists in Maycomb." Pause. "Hence, learning about racism is a loss of her innocence, when she's grown up in such a sheltered world."

Although, in and of itself, she gets to learn about it, instead of experiencing it. The black characters evidently didn't get to enjoy that innocence or really, ignorance—when it comes to racism—in the first place.

"Well said," Ms. Daniels nods, and I think I'm out of the woods when, "How do you personally feel about Lee's take on racism and ignorance in the novel?" Her eyes bore into mine, and I feel my heart skip in my chest.

Well, it's hard for me to unhear the way the n-word was said dozens upon dozens upon dozens of times throughout the novel. It's hard for me to unsee how undeveloped and ignored Tom Robinson's character was. How he died, and that was it.

It's hard for me to forget how Calpurnia could've said more, *shown* more. How she'd claimed that 'colored' people chose not to learn how to speak properly, despite the fact that it had been illegal for us to even get educated and learn how to read.

It's hard for me to see Atticus as the perfect, flawless savior who could do no wrong, and could only put his reputation on the line for the unfortunate Tom Robinson.

I bite my lip.

"I thought it was a unique take on racism for the time period it was released in." I finally say.

Ms. Daniels won't stop though, "Any personal takes?" She turns to the class, "There's some controversy surrounding whether or not the book should still be taught in schools, and there's varying opinions surrounding what message Lee is sending readers about racism." She turns to me, "I'd love to see more of your take on this, Amina."

The eyes start to feel like they're burning into my flesh. I feel ghost bugs crawling up my skin. I can already hear the implicit, "because you're black," at the end of her suggestion.

"I guess Lee was very focused on the characterization of characters such as Atticus and Scout, more so than other characters," I say. The main characters, albeit, but not the ones on the receiving end of the racism.

The black characters; the ones who were facing oppression were the *other characters* that went uncharacterized.

I don't say that, though.

"Can you list some examples?" Ms. Daniels asks, leaning forward in her seat.

Daniels really woke up and chose violence today. I exhale, tucking a braid behind my ear. "Uh... Tom Robinson... Calpurnia—when it comes to their own personal takes and experiences of racism."

"So..." One of Brett's lackeys cut in, "The black ones?"

My shoulders fall into a shrug while my face burns.

"Well," Ms. Daniels starts, in the way of someone who asks you a question, but doesn't truly want your answer, "the readers were given the opportunity to understand that Tom Robinson was a good man. He went out of his way to help Mayella Ewell for no other reason but good morals."

I mull my choice of words in my head before starting slowly, "He was vaguely described as a good person throughout the novel. Although, it would've been interesting to actually see his point of view, seeing as he was the one accused. Maybe some more experiences in his life outside of Mayella Ewell."

Now, it's hard for me to stop, "He also inexplicably tried to run away from jail, essentially killing himself," Ms. Daniels purses her lips and I find myself continuing.

"It just seemed really out of character. I mean, from the little they gave us of his character," I give a small, dry smile, "He had a wife and three children that he loved deeply and he was careful throughout everything, you know? It just seems odd that all of a sudden he just wouldn't care anymore and put everything on the line. He seemed like the type to wait it out, even though he was in awful conditions." I lean forward in my chair, "He was hopeful before, right? Then all of a sudden he wasn't. He put everything on the line when he tried to escape, despite the fact that he had to have known he couldn't have gotten out alive when it was a prison with massive walls and a multitude of guards," I pause, "So, what happened between the court case and his death? Did something in jail change his mind or heighten his desperation all of a sudden? If so, wouldn't it have been great for Lee to give us insight into that?"

Murmurs fill the classroom. I'm talking way more than I'm supposed to, way more than I allow myself to.

"And all of a sudden, Lee leaves us with this final message that implies that Atticus did all he could, but instead of waiting out his sentence, Tom Robinson decided to run away from those clearly impossible conditions. So, at the end of the day, *To Kill A Mockingbird* leaves us by giving readers the impression that there wasn't much hope for Robinson in the first place, and everything goes back to normal, without an in-depth look into Tom Robinson's mind." I can feel a subtle shakiness creeping into my voice. I clear my throat,

"Then we get some mini conversation with Boo Radley, another person tied to the theme of killing innocence... and then that's it. It's over." My voice softens to barely a whisper. "I guess what I'm saying is that I would've loved to see some more in depth characterization of Tom Robinson and any other characters like him, seeing as *To Kill A Mockingbird* is a book revolving around the anti-black racism that was prominent. Yet, we're not exactly seeing anything from the point of view of any of the oppressed in this case."

Silence answers me.

Everyone's eyes are boring into me, from the sketchy kids in the back to the bubbly girls in front, to Brett's lackeys. My gaze drifts to Ms. Daniels whose eyebrows are raised.

"Well," She clears her throat, "That's certainly one take on the novel."

One take. Somehow, I hear *the wrong take.* I sink back into my chair, as though if I sink far enough, I might just disappear and save myself from this painfully awkward situation, and from Ms. Daniels, who probably hates me at this point.

After an uncomfortable few moments, the conversation sways back to themes and symbolism. My little speech is brushed right back under the rug, and Scout's innocence is the topic that dominates the rest of the class.

When the bell rings, I can't get out of the classroom fast enough. Well, that's until Ms. Daniels calls my name and I actually feel my stomach drop to the floor. I turn to her, books still firmly tucked under my arms, backpack hanging from my shoulders.

"You seemed a bit stressed out today," She says, slowly, adjusting her reading glasses.

"Um, I'm not really stressed," I reply, giving her a slow nod and a strained smile.

"Well, you can always see the counsellor if you're feeling bothered." She says, kind of ignoring what I just said.

I just nod because there's no point in me telling her that the counsellor doesn't even know my name and in the few instances that I *do* interact with Mrs. Clark, she's always telling me about universities that don't require AP courses, despite the fact that I'm already taking some APs this year. Not only that, but I'm still flying by in As and

A-plusses that prove that a decade of Kumon and sweat-inducing effort has paid off. So, taking APs isn't something I'm planning on avoiding, especially if I'm planning on getting out of here for college. Meet up with my brother, possibly.

"Anything else?" She asks.

"I think I'm good," I reply, gently.

Her gaze holds mine for a moment. "Alright, have a good afternoon."

"You too," I say, carefully turning on my heel and heading out of the classroom.

While leaving, I pretend I don't feel the calculating eyes of one Ms. Daniels burning into my back.

not a rebel

"What happened during English class?"

The voice stops me right in my tracks, and I whip around to see three of the girls that run the school. Well, somewhat.

Amber, Leslie, and Olivia. Or, ALO as I've christened them as.

I honestly forget who is who sometimes.

Their hair colours vary slightly, I guess. Amber's sporting some shade of tawny. Leslie has dark brown hair that stops right above her waist. Olivia has some sort of red tinge to her hair.

Amber asks the question, standing right in the middle of the sidewalk directly outside the school, gusts of wind billowing our hair and skirts.

Amber Wesley. I let out an amused gust of air. Amber Wesley is the type of person that claps every time a plane lands, the type that always makes sure to let her listener know that her eyes change colors, (which they don't), and the type that talks to her bad hair days by comparing them to black hair. (i.e.*"Ew, my hair is so freakin' frizzy today. It looks like an Afro."* Usually followed by an exaggerated sigh, as she runs her hands through greasy waves *"I want to* delete *my existence.")* The type that starts awkward sentences with: *"not to sound racist, but—"*

"Um," I shift my weight to the side, pulling myself out of my thoughts. "Nothing much?"

I'm actually surprised the trio knows that I exist. I mean, I guess it's hard to ignore the only black girl in the entire school, but most people do a pretty good job of doing so.

"Well, John told us you had a little freak-out during the class discussion." This time it's Leslie, carefully pulling her ridiculously long hair into a ponytail.

My mind slowly attempts to register her comment. Because I never once raised my voice. In fact, I made sure that my tone stayed even and calm throughout the entire time I spoke.

I shake my head. "I didn't."

"He should've taken a video," Amber mutters, shaking her head at her friends.

"What was the whole thing about, anyways?" Olivia asks.

"*To Kill A Mockingbird*," I say, carefully glancing between the three girls. They exchange glances and I take that opportunity to start heading home, "Anyway, I've got to get going."

"Wait," Amber asks, hazel eyes burning into my skin.

I pause, drawing my mouth into a line.

"You could sit with us at lunch tomorrow, if you want." Leslie proposes, re-adjusting her ponytail for what looks like the millionth time.

I almost let out a laugh at the proposition. *They're kidding.* Just the thought of me sitting at a table surrounded by ALO and Brett's group of White Bros™ makes me feel like either throwing up or just laughing at the absurdity of it all.

"I—I'll think about it," I finally get out. I'm ready to be completely done with this conversation when Olivia speaks up again, hands resting on her hips.

"Not to put any pressure on you or anything, but Mrs. Clark is kind of concerned about your well-being and asked us," She gestures between the three of them, "to take you in."

There it is.

Leslie gives my shoulder an awkward squeeze. "It's not like a charity case thing." It kind of looks like that's exactly what it is. "*Though*, it would look good for Amber's StuCo campaign, and it'll help us *all* get into Mrs. Clark's good books."

I give her a slow nod.

"For the record, this doesn't have anything to do with the fact that you're..." She pauses, eyes roving over me. "Well." Amber finishes awkwardly, giving me a dainty smile, and informing me that it most likely has everything to do with my dark skin.

Their choice to recruit the only black girl in the entire school most likely has something to do with my race. The fact that Amber deemed it necessary to assure me that it didn't only strengthens my assumption.

Olivia speaks up. "They're also taking another picture for the school website, and the principal wants you in it."

"It'll be fun," Leslie grins, "Like a little photoshoot."

I bite my bottom lip.

I'm guessing Emory is going to be a part of the picture, and Yasmine, too. Not to mention a couple of the Asians from the Asian/Gamer table.

And that essentially makes up all the non-white people in this school.

Of course, it's *purely* coincidental. Purely coincidental that 93% of the student body is white, and the 7% of everyone else is just *coincidentally* going to be in the shoot.

Purely coincidental that the representation is bound to make Elkwood look like the most diverse school in the state.

"Um, yeah. Sure. Maybe," I manage to get out.

"We'll see you at lunch tomorrow," Amber says, then winks. "*Maybe.*"

I try to quash down my embarrassment as I hold onto the straps of my backpack, keeping my head down as I turn on my heel and speed down the sidewalks, willing myself to get home as fast as possible.

***

Walking home has always spiked my nerves. Sometimes it's peaceful, other times my anxiety sky-rockets.

It probably doesn't help that the first time I walked home from school, I got lost. I'd ended up at a house that definitely wasn't my parents'. When a random couple had opened the door, I'd ended up murmuring some apologies before heading on my way.

However, I was *lucky* enough to run into some officer on duty. He asked me a ton of questions, had a vice-like grip on my arm. Any answer I gave him didn't suffice, and he never stopped looming over me, never stopped grabbing onto me, leaving bruises.

Afternoon melted into night, and that's when he received a call from my parents who were worried out of their minds.

I tilt my head to the side, my backpack swinging behind me as I kick at some pebbles on the sidewalk.

So, the officer drove me home, and I was shaking, *literally* shaking throughout the entire ride. When he dropped me off, he left me with a light warning.

Despite my mom attempting to gently explain the situation, no progress was truly made. After all, we didn't belong.

We'd only moved to the neighborhood that year.

A dry laugh escapes my lips as I carefully cross the street, my shoes padding across a familiar path. The memory punctures through the air once more.

"Just wanted to make sure that there wasn't anything off," He had said to my parents with that patronizing half-grin that I've grown to recognize in this town.

Although, I always wonder how he saw any danger through the anxious tears streaming down my cheeks.

My house comes into view in its full ivory glory, and I walk up the front steps.

Slipping my key out of my back pocket, I unlock the front door.

I push it open, walking into the mahogany floored, lemon scented house that I've gotten used to over the past few years. Sure, experiences outside of the white villa have been pretty awful, but this is my home.

Running my hand across the walls, I kick the door shut behind me as I make my way towards the kitchen.

When I'm home, I can sing at the top of my lungs, fling myself onto my bed as music swirls in the air. I can breathe, let my breaths slip from my lips like wind, create playlists as my thoughts flow like currents.

As soon as I step through that white doorway, I'm untouchable.

Heading further into the kitchen, I rummage through the fridge. I end up making myself a bowl of cereal, taking a seat in the living room as I start to grab everything I need from my backpack.

The conversation that I had with ALO plays in my head over and over again. I shuffle through the sheets of paper, wondering if I was right about the school photo being some sort of diversity project. I'd ask the other people of color in the school, but we don't necessarily talk.

Setting my cereal aside, I place some finishing strokes on my art project, letting my playlist fill the air as I layer stroke upon stroke. A few minutes later, I set the canvas aside, biting back a smile at my final painting, resisting the urge to layer more strokes because of how therapeutic it is.

Then, I'm grabbing my laptop from the floor and I start to type away, letting paragraphs upon paragraphs form on my screen. An essay for English. One that Ms. Daniels assigned the class before it all went to hell.

The essay to be flawless. Elkwood doesn't do subpar, and if you're me, mediocrity is never an option. Ms. Clark doesn't need any proof to doubt me more than she already does.

At my last click, I hear the garage door opening, making my head shoot up.

In a second, I rise to my feet, making my way to the front door as it's pulled open, opening my mouth to say just about a million things.

***

"So," Dad's laugh echoes throughout the house, "They're using y'all to look more diverse?"

I drop my fork into my plate, raising a hand, "that's *exactly* what I thought."

We're all seated around the table, forks stabbing into pasta and glasses being raised to our lips every so often. Both of my parents are seated across from me, home from work, and my younger sister's seated right next to me, finally home after a day of school.

"Diversity's nice," Mom says from next to Dad, "but I'm not a big fan of using the non-white students as some sort of prop to aid that image." She continues, black-as-night braids piled into a bun, Dad making a murmur of agreement.

"Especially since Elkwood is *really* racist," My younger sister cuts in, grinning cheekily through bites of pasta.

Mom laughs, tucking a beaded braid behind the 8-year-old's ear. "Who told you that?"

"I just... I just *know,*" Claudette emphasizes, giving us a knowing nod. "Plus," She starts after a few moments, "You only let Amina go to Elkwood. Not me."

Dad exchanges glances with Mom in the briefest of looks. "Well," He says, "Elkwood's also expensive."

Claudie shrugs, poking a fork back in her macaroni, not knowing how right on the mark she was.

My parents seem less than eager to rush Claudie into Elkwood. After all, it's competitive, an environment that can suck the life out of bright eyes.

I mean, Claudie'll eventually have to go to Elkwood, but before she has to volunteer as tribute, she gets to relax in a public school for a couple more years.

It'll be a better fit for her. The issues in Elkwood essentially surround race and class; two things that go hand in hand more often than not. So, Claudie's better off by avoiding being thrust into that world too quickly. Or ever.

I shake my head, turning back to my parents, "We talked about *To Kill A Mockingbird,* today."

"Oh," Dad chuckles, twirling his fork, "That's great."

"Yeah. It was absolutely fantastic," I say, echoing his tone as he exhales another laugh.

I lean forward in my chair. "Ms. Daniels asked me for my personal opinion on the novel and she wasn't too happy with my response."

Mom rubs her temples with a short laugh. "What did you say to her?"

"Uh, I kind of rambled about some of the issues in the way Lee portrayed race relations and the lack of characterization for the black characters." I play around with my fingers, glancing at them with a semi-apologetic look.

Claudie looks up, fishing her fork out of her pasta. "You've done it now," she shakes her head at me, not having any idea what we're talking about.

I raise my hand to my chest in faux offense, and she scrunches her nose at me.

"I mean, I didn't raise my voice or anything." I say, turning to my parents.

Dad leans back in his chair. "Well, that's good."

"Yeah," Mom purses her lips at me, "We want you to talk, okay?" she leans forward, one of those faint grins on her lips. "Just," a pause as she tilts her head to the side, eyes softening, "be cautious and thoughtful."

"I know," I say with a nod.

"I mean, some teachers in Elkwood aren't your *biggest* fans." Dad says, giving me a half smile.

"You sure?" I snort, Dad cracking one of those wide grins that he claims I stole from his gene pool. Wide, and hal- dimpled, stretching across his face like the sun.

"*So*, we don't want to give them even the slightest excuse to try and target you," Mom adds, giving me a soft smile. It's semi-apologetic, as though any of this is her fault.

"Got it." I say, fingers gently drumming the table as I attempt to quirk a grin.

"You only have two more years here, alright?" A wink. "You've got this." Mom says, holding out her glass for Dad as he pours sparkling apple juice into it.

The bottle is passed around the table, and a few seconds later, all our cups are filled to the rim with the golden juice. Dad raises his glass, and the rest of us raise our glasses to his with a *clink*.

Mom meets each of our eyes. "To another year at Elkwood."

"To another year at Elkwood," The rest of us echo, and seconds later, I'm raising my drink to my lips, letting the apple sweetness dominate my mouth and erase everything else but this moment in time.

raceless crime

"I'm about to blow your mind," Mr. Pham says, pacing the front of the classroom, a self-satisfied grin curling onto his lips. As usual, Debate with Mr. Pham is bound to be a trip.

Sweatshirts are already on, glasses, beanies and baseball hats perched on the top of heads, and hair is lazily straying into the air or tucked behind ears.

Debate topics dominate the rest of what Mr. Pham goes on to say, and students stay leaning against counters, quiet conversations arising here and there.

Mr. Pham is probably the only teacher at Elkwood who isn't completely white. With a white mother, and a Vietnamese father, he technically fits into the multiracial category. His hair is dark brown, almost-black, and he sports features that carry both aspects of his identity. I'd say he passes, though. People might blink, but they won't look twice at him when he walks through the halls.

Mr. Pham's nice. Nice in the way that makes you lightly chuckle at his easy jokes. Nice in the way that makes you almost want to approach him when you have a question. Nice in the way he has a constant grin that seems to never leave his face. Just *nice*.

Debate is technically an extracurricular, and my parents essentially coerced me into joining, because "colleges like that." Sure, debate class fuels my already high anxiety levels, but maybe it'll all be worth it come graduation.

I glance over at two girls silently giggling at something on one of their phones. My gaze returns to the front.

At least, I hope it'll all be worth it.

Mr. Pham's gaze drifts over us. "You'll need someone to research with, so..." I wince, knowing exactly what two words are coming next.

"Pair up."

Pairing up at Elkwood is a ritual. As in, there's a process to it. A systemic, step-by-step process. Something that I still haven't completely grasped in my fourth year of going here.

To me, it's a blur of glances, sidles, handshakes, nods, gestures and beckons, too quick and too subtle for me to even process. So, I watch everything occur, helplessly, too awkward to ask, and too uncomfortable to try.

"Who doesn't have a partner?" Mr. Pham asks, and the awkwardness shrivels in my chest like bad fruit.

I raise an awkward hand.

"I can..." People's eyes lazily drift to me, "I can work by myself."

A hum, Mr. Pham's head tilts to the side, lips pursing. "Uh, how about you pair up with one of those boys?" He asks, and I wince.

My gaze drifts over to them, and sure enough, he's referring to the White Bros™. Well, two of them, plus the singular black boy in the school. One Emory Richards.

"You're a group of three. One of you can pair up with Amina." Two of the guys glance at each other, then their gazes dart to different parts of the classroom.

Emory lets out a breath before shuffling towards me.

"Great," Mr. Pham snaps his fingers with a grin, "Emory will pair up with you."

Emory towers over me once he's made his way to my side, laptop in hand.

Mr. Pham double claps. "Get to work."

As class resumes, I spare a glance at Emory who places his laptop on the table, fingers flying across the keyboard.

I glance at the sheet in hand. "Our topic is um, social issues."

Emory purses his lips, still typing at the laptop. I pull out my own, setting it on the table next to his.

I slide my notebook out, eyes still roving over the sheet. "So, we can delve into topics like poverty, drug abuse, prostitution..." I pause at the last question before reciting slowly, "racial discrimination."

At this, Emory finally looks over at me with chestnut brown eyes. "Fun." He says.

Real fun.

"So... which ones are you researching about?" I ask, voice careful.

"I'll tackle poverty and prostitution." He says, eyes returning back to his laptop.

Leaving *me* with drug abuse and racial discrimination. Shout-out to Emory for leaving me with the best topics.

My lips purse. Not like his topics are any better, though. Issues are issues.

Our work time passes in silence, save for the occasional notebook scribbles. We don't talk much, just make clarifications every once in a while.

By the time debate passes by, we have a page full of evidence and sources, details and highlighted notes.

"Alright, alright." Mr. Pham grins from the front. "Hopefully, you all got some work done. If we have time... " He glances at his watch, "*or* next class, we'll go around and review our notes and information, sharing it with the group. And in a couple of weeks, Ms. Wilson and I will be administering a debate during your history class. Should be fun."

I trill my lips. *That should be a trip.*

The bell rings. Mr. Pham clasps his hands together, "See you all next week."

I shuffle with my supplies, shoving it into my backpack.

A thin smile curves onto Emory's lips. He opens his mouth to say something, but is caught off by Brett beckoning for him to come over to where the White Bros™ are standing.

Emory glances over at him for a moment before his gaze returns to me. "See you next class." He finally says before whipping around in the direction of Brett and his friends, only looking back once.

"Yeah," I say, several beats too late, as I watch them all retreat from the classroom, "See you."

***

The juice place.

Brightly coloured fruity drinks, ice cold blocks floating in each smoothie, and a multitude of teens in the magenta and olive green juicery that's arguably the centerpiece of the town.

I tend to avoid it like the plague.

The juice place means ALO, it means the White Bros™ and essentially means other teenagers, all of which are problematic for my mental health.

The only reason I've stepped *foot* in here is due to the fact that some girl in Claudie's class is having a party here this Friday evening. It starts in about an hour or so, but I have to watch Claudie until then, due to the fact that my parents are working.

So, I'm here, trying to convince my little sister to wait for juice, even though I know that I'm already going to end up buying her one before the juice-themed party starts.

"I want the pomegranate one," Claudie says, pointing towards the juice counter before adjusting her baby blue dress.

"And you'll get it once What's-Her-Face's party starts," I reply.

Claudie gives me an unimpressed look. "Her name is *Angie*." She shakes her head, letting out an exaggerated groan. "We've been over this a million times."

I laugh. "Attitude."

"It's only because I want juice," Claudie bats her eyelashes, swinging her tiny feet back and forth.

I let out a breath, shaking my head as I cave in. "Only one."

I'm so weak.

Claudie cheers in response, and I roll my eyes at her, rising to my feet and heading to the front.

In line, I fumble through my backpack, slipping out a wrinkled five dollar bill for one of the overpriced drinks.

The line's getting shorter, and I wait in line, humming to myself, my eyes drifting around the juicery.

My heart almost skips a beat when they walk in. All of them. The entire posse, consisting of Brett and a couple of friends, alongside ALO and one or two others. Some of them are still decked out in schoolwear, others just dressed casually as they walk into the juicery. Not that I'm surprised that they're here; it would've honestly been more surprising if they weren't. It's an Elkwood teenager tradition; coming here after school.

That being said, I still can't say that my nerves don't spike ever-so-slightly.

Amber's the first to notice me. "I'm seeing you everywhere," She laughs light, syrupy laughter. "I didn't even know you knew this place existed."

I try to smile. I mean, it'd be hard not to run into her, given that the town isn't massive. Plus, everyone in Elkwood knows that the juicery exists. I choose not to go for various reasons, one of which being having this current conversation.

"Kidding," She says with that grossly sweet smile.

Emory's eyes meet mine for a second, giving me a brief nod before delving back into conversation with Brett and his followers.

Leslie appears on my right. "So, the photo?"

The line is still getting shorter, and I shrug. "Still thinking about it."

Olivia claps twice, and glances at me with the dark freckles dotting her face. "Well, think quickly."

I hum, and my gaze drifts to the front as the line shortens.

"I mean, everyone's been selected, so it's not like it's really up to choice," Amber chirps, ever-so-straight to the point.

"Right," I say.

"Well, not everyone," It's Brett, and our eyes drift to him as I remember that he's still here.

"No one in our group is in the photo," He says, and the White Bros™ give affirmative grunts as my eyebrows knit together.

"I'm calling racism," One says, earning a chuckle from the girls and the rest of his group, save for Emory who suddenly looks invested in his Nikes.

"Yeah," Brett agrees, "There are barely any white people in the shoot," He says, glancing towards me. The girls let out low giggles, Olivia biting her bottom lip.

Amber's eyes widen in amusement as she eyes me from the corner of her eye, "*Brett*."

He shrugs. "It's true." Then his eyes widen in faux shock, "Or am I not allowed to say that?"

"Leslie's in it," Olivia cuts in, nodding towards the brunette who wiggles her fingers in a wave.

"Alright, well, I'm calling racism and sexism, then." He decides, the smug grin refusing to drop from his face.

"People get butthurt and all of a sudden, *we* get brushed off to the side." His friend adds, gesturing among them.

"Well, except Emory." Another says, chuckles breaking out into the air as Emory's lips are pulled into a line.

Brett nudges him. "It's a joke, *man*." I mirror Emory's nearly imperceptible wince at the word. Brett plows on, "but, you've got to admit it."

Emory lets out a dry chuckle. "Admit what?"

"Elkwood's trying so hard to be 'woke' that they're starting to discriminate against us." Pause. "Well, not you, but *us*."

Emory raises his eyebrows.

"You honestly can't say anything anymore." Brett is on a roll, unwilling to stop. "Like, if I decided to talk about black on black crime for example..." Brett rolls his eyes, tilting his head back. "Emory, don't look at me like that. I'm just stating my opinion."

Emory isn't really looking at him in any particular way. Really, the only sign of annoyance on Emory's features is his slightly raised eyebrows.

"Anyways," Brett continues, "If I were to talk about that, everyone would be on me like I'm racist."

Two people are left in front of me in the line, and I'm honestly ready for the ground to swallow me up and never spit me back out. Heat creeps onto my face, travels throughout my body, Brett's smug smile only seems to be getting bigger.

Don't say anything, Amina.

Don't say anything—

"I mean, I think it's because the term black on black crime doesn't really make sense if you think about it."

I almost think the words are coming out of my mouth when I see her, hair pulled back into a low ponytail, stance relaxed. The girl has two cups of juice in hand, and my gaze drifts to the back where someone—I'm guessing an older sister— is watching the interaction unfold.

I'm still trying to wrap my head around why Yasmine Abadi is here.

Yasmine and I don't interact. We just *don't.* It's not hatred that keeps us apart, merely distance. We have exactly zero classes together and our paths never seem to collide. Instead, we almost weave around each other, twisting into our own separate universes.

"What are you getting at, Abadi?" There are creases in Brett's eyebrows as he pushes a wave out of his hair. "That black people aren't killing each other in urban areas?" And the rest of the guys laugh at the question while I try not to physically cringe at his words. My attempt is unsuccessful.

Yasmine shrugs, tilting her head to the side. "Dude, I'm getting at the fact that a white person is really just as likely to kill another white person as a black person is likely to kill another black person." She purses her lips, eyes steady on him, ever the model UN member.

A scoff escapes Brett's lips. A signature scoff that people like Brett return to any valid argument, essentially telling their opposer that they're inherently wrong no matter how many facts they dish out.

Really, someone like Brett could be confronted with all sorts of statistics and scoff it off, because he can. Because someone told him he can. My skin crawls.

"If you look at the stats, " I find myself saying, even though I should really just shut up. I'm tempted to implore the universe to backspace my existence. *Just ctrl alt delete*, "people killing other people of the same race is common. It's the default. It's just crime."

"No strings attached." Yasmine says, nodding.

"Right," Brett easily drags the word on. A smug grin tugs at his lips. He seems far too arrogant to be legal.

I try not to let it get to me.

"Using the term black on black crime is just ignorant." Yasmine grins lightly. "Just my opinion, though."

"Oh, I'm ignorant?" Brett laughs. He glances about his group of friends. "Hate to break it to you, but some of us look at actual stats instead of Twitter."

"The term implies," I continue gently as though Brett hasn't interrupted, "that black people are killing other people for the sole reason of them being black." I pause. "That isn't true, though. Black people are more likely to live around black people, and the same goes with every other race."

When Mr. Pham said debate was something that we're encouraged to do and "jump at" even outside of school, the thought never occurred to me that I'd be right here engaging in an actual debate with some members of the debate team.

It's strange enough that I've even said a *word.*

"Hence," Yasmine adds, "There's a higher likelihood of altercations within the same race. So, it's just crime." Another shrug. She lifts one shoulder, lets it fall. "I mean, people of the same race are more likely to kill people of the *same* race. Statistically proven." A polite laugh escapes her lips. "Makes sense, though, doesn't it?"

"So, really," I start slowly, "what you call black on black crime is comparable; well, actually equivalent to what no one calls white-on-white crime." I finish, watching glances exchange and eyes blink.

Brett glances around, exchanging that smug gust of air with his friends, as all great debaters do when confronted with evidence that counters their claim. "Right," he says, as though trying to placate an infant.

"Throw the whole term away," Yasmine shrugs, grabbing two straws. "Makes no sense whatsoever. Crime within the same race is just that; crime. No one race is more violent, and spreading misinformation just adds pointless racist connotations." A pause and a careful smile. "Something that we don't really need right now."

I find my lungs suddenly functioning, my breaths escaping my lips while Yasmine grins at all of us, saying, "Well, that's just my two cents. This was nice." Another grin. "Have a good one," before making her way over to her older sister who immediately starts shooting out questions, her gaze wandering to us before returning back to her sister.

The last person in front of me finally grabs their drink and leaves, while I ask the person in front for a pomegranate drink for Claudie.

"I barely understood what she was trying to say," I hear one of Brett's friends chuckle, eliciting laughter from the rest of them. Amber, Leslie and Olivia sprinkle some polite laughter as the person in front slides my drink over to me.

Yasmine Abadi really spelt it out for them in the simplest way possible. However, I allow them to laugh it off outside, while their minds churn with the words that have punctured through the air.

Grabbing my drink from the floor, I place the five dollar bill in the cashier's hand and wait to receive change.

My mind's turning, too, potent questions ringing in my head. I'm certain Yasmine knew exactly what she was doing as she diplomatically slipped seeds of thoughts into our minds. With that, I blink a couple of times, trying to shake a few of the thoughts away.

The cashier hands me the change, and I murmur a quick, "thank you," as I grab the juice and head out of the lunch line.

Claudie's eyes light up when she sees her drink. I slide it over to her with a straw.

"That took *forever*." She groans.

My eyes narrow at her, and she beams at me, innocently. "Thanks, Amina."

I hum, shaking my head at her as the minutes tick away to her friend's birthday party.

She takes a long slurp out of the juice. "How come it took so long, anyway?"

I shrug, gaze drifting to Emory who's seated at the table with the rest of his supposed friends, all being rowdy, along with the girls who are hovering around their table, smirks sliding onto their faces. Emory's eyes meet mine for half a second before his gaze flits away, so quickly I could've sworn I'd imagined it.

My gaze drifts away from their table, and I squint, catching the eye of Yasmine who's seated across the juicery. She throws me a smile that I hesitantly return.

I turn back to my sister, whose warm brown eyes are still on me. I shrug once more.

"Just a long line."

racist-dar

Have you ever walked into a place that just *feels* racist? I'm certain every black person has quite a few key things in common. And one of the most fundamental attributes that I'm sure we all share is the uncanny ability to detect a racist from miles away.

Maybe it's DNA. Maybe it's instinct. All I know is that from the age of six, I could detect a racist; hell, I could tell if someone was racist even if *they* didn't know they were racist.

At times, it only takes a glance for me to know.

I've never been one for superstition, but this is a sixth sense that I've never questioned. Sure, you can't tell solely by looks, but really, it's the aura that racists give off. A cold aura. In simple words: they do not pass the vibe check.

Some people make it extremely obvious, what with the hostile glares, gross sneers, or supercilious smirks. Sometimes it's the person that constantly casts you weary looks, maybe crosses to the other side of the road. The difficult ones? The ones that are smiling. With every interaction, thin lips are pulled into a tight beam, with nods every so often. The only way you can know for sure when it comes to those people is by analyzing how fake the smile is, or realizing that after your interaction, you feel worse than you did before going in.

Right now, as I stand in the middle of the store, a shopping bag slung over my elbow, my racist-dar buffers as it tries to determine whether or not the brunette who's standing off to the side is just observing me, or scouting me with distrust.

Going outside has never been my thing. Or maybe it was, back when I was a blissful six-year-old who tried to make conversation with every stranger she walked past. Well, now, that little girl is a slightly uncomfy 16-year-old and is more than anxious to step out of the doors of her house. Yeah, I *am* a homebody. And yeah, it's probably unhealthy.

My main concern at the moment is getting my hands on a new pair of sneakers for P.E. Mom was supposed to help me look for the new sneakers, but she got called in for an impromptu meeting with some colleagues, so here I am; alone in the sneaker place, attempting to buy some sneakers before gym class next Monday.

"You're practically grown now," Mom had said while dropping me off. "I'm pretty sure you're capable of buying a pair of shoes. It's not rocket science."

"We can do it next week," I had offered, standing next to the car and feeling more than vulnerable in the empty parking lot.

"We can't. Have you seen the state of your current sneakers? They won't make it through next gym class."

"Mom," I had exhaled a pleading gust of air. "Can we not? Please?"

Mom had only laughed in response before driving off.

Now, in the shoe shop, I'm divided between a pair of sneakers, both of them happening to be almost identical to my previous ones.

From the corner of my eye, I feel the brunette's eyes stay on me as her feet start tapping on the floor. She has a tag and a vest identical to everyone who works here.

Her eyes are beady.

I hold the two pairs of shoes up in front of me. Then I slip my phone out of my pocket, taking pictures of each to send to Mom.

"Excuse me?" The brunette approaches me, one finger raised in the air.

My heart skips as it often does in situations like these, situations when my heart starts pounding and my chest starts constricting.

"Yes?" I ask, freezing in place.

"Are you buying those?" She asks. Her voice is nasally, almost irritable to my ears, but I give her a hesitant smile anyway.

"Um, one of them." I say, glancing between the two of them.

"Why are you taking pictures of them?" She asks. A mother and daughter pass by us, glancing over at the two of us before averting their gazes.

My eyes find a middle-aged redhead towards the back, happily taking pictures of different TV sets, fingers furiously flying across her phone as she proceeds to take more pictures.

The brunette's question seems more than unnecessary.

"T-to send to my mom." I mentally curse myself for stuttering, "I'm sending her the options since she's busy at the moment."

Discomfort curls at my insides.

The brunette raises her eyebrows.

"Well, you're not buying both of them, are you?" She asks, beady eyes tracing the shoes.

"Just one of them," I say, just like I told her just moments ago.

"I still don't understand why you need to take pictures." She says. I glance at her.

I still don't understand why she thinks it's such a big deal when this shop doesn't have a policy against this, when other shoppers are doing the same thing without qualms.

"I'm going to buy one of these," I say, slowly.

"Okay," She gives me that patronizing grin, taking a few steps back. "Just keeping the store safe."

Freezing, I carefully glance around the store. A multitude of things run through my mind at her last statement.

A chill flies down my spine when I realize that it's not just her.

A kid decked out in a plain t-shirt and shorts gives me an unwavering look, tapping his Dad's shoulder. His dad turns around, narrowing his eyes at me, and I take note of the MAGA hat perched upon his head.

My heart starts running a marathon, and the back of my neck burns.

A lady off to the side quirks her eyebrows at me in utter indignance, looking just about ready to ask: *Is there a problem here?*

My eyes dart to a somewhat short man, potbelly peeking out of his wife beater, hands calloused, face sunburnt, eyes frigid and angry, Confederate handkerchief peeking out of his vest.

You're okay, Amina.

You're okay.

Unfortunately, my anxiety disagrees.

My hands tremble as the brunette that works in the store still stares me down, the faintest of smirks touching her lips, as if to say: *you're in my territory.*

And all the unfriendly, distrustful faces remind me of one policeman on one autumn afternoon, one intense grab of my 12-year old wrist. It reminds me of Mrs. Clark, and her passive aggressive hatred towards me, it reminds me of the cafeteria and the walk of shame to my table, trying to avoid all the faces.

My hands refuse to stop trembling.

With quickening breaths, my eyes dart to my phone. Mom hasn't responded about the shoe options yet. She's likely to be busy, anyway.

My nerves steadily but surely rise as I feel the lady watching me, arms casually crossed.

Deep breath in, deep breath out.

I carefully return one shoe box, placing the other shoes back into their own shoe box and tucking it under my arm.

I make my way through the store, and the woman tails behind me throughout. Passerbys' eyes drift to us, and I feel heat consume my insides.

As I go down one aisle, she follows. I retrace my steps, she follows. I turn up the next aisle, she's right behind me.

The last thing I want to do right now is draw attention. However, apparently I'm a beacon, something that doesn't help with the brunette following me everywhere I go.

So, I hunch my shoulders over, eyes trailing the floor as I make my way to the line, shoe box clutched in hands.

The brunette doesn't follow me into the line, but stands off to the side, glasses glinting underneath the luminous lights as her eyes cut harshly into my skin.

I fumble for my money at the counter, and the woman's eyes narrow. The cashier slides my change over to me, and shoves my shoe box to me, so quickly that it almost hits the floor before I catch it.

"Thank you," I get out, almost inaudibly. No response.

I still feel the woman's eyes on my back as I lean against the escalator, sending a text to my mom instead of calling her, because if she hears my voice, I know she'll be able to hear the ugly patheticness building up in my chest, I know she'll be able to hear that my voice sounds like glass, ready to break at any given moment. I know she'll hear my *hurt*, and I can't afford that.

So, I text.

When Mom's car pulls onto the front of the mall, and she rolls down the windows with a big grin, I give it my all to return her smile.

Although, when I pull myself into the car, seated next to her, a shoe box clutched in my hands, I let out a shaky breath.

Four years in the little Midwestern town Elkwood, and this still ruins me. Meanwhile, there are still other issues in the back of my mind like my counselor, the photograph, and the unwarranted lunch invitation from girls that would never look twice at me on a daily basis.

"Baby, are you okay?" I barely hear Mom's voice through the pounding in my head. My head pounds harder, my heart clenches painfully.

Then, I break down.

lunch with the girls

The cafeteria is chaos.

Not like it's anything abnormal. As usual, lunch is dominated by the yells of a hundred or so teenagers, the clashing sounds of trays being dropped on tables, (or the floor if you're unlucky enough), the sound of people clapping once a tray falls to the ground, spilling its contents. It's a cacophony of the clashes, the laughs, and the yells.

I'm too used to it to be bothered.

Once I leave the lunch line, tray in hand, I make my way over to the back of the cafeteria, where my empty table is calling my name.

I'm almost at the table when I hear my name being called from a different direction.

"Amina!"

I whip in the direction to see Amber, Leslie, and Olivia waving their hands in the air, gesturing for me to sit at their table. A string of curses flies through my mind. I've been able to avoid sitting with them since their offer last week, but now, I've been found.

I glance around the cafeteria, and see people's eyes drift to me, and then to ALO, back and forth like they can't comprehend what they're seeing.

I can't comprehend it, either. Well, I didn't comprehend it at first, until I realized that I was a charity case to get ALO in Mrs. Clark's good books, and a prop to help Amber's campaign for StuCo. Reaching out to isolated, (*minority*) students looks good on a college resume, I guess.

If I can just pretend I can't hear or see them, it'll be great. I've managed to skirt past their lunch invitation for the past week, and I think I've been doing a decent job. Although, now, called out in the middle of the cafeteria, all eyes on me, it's hard for me to duck back into the shadows.

Or, really, virtually impossible.

Brett narrows his eyes as I shuffle over to their table, in the way I would imagine my ancestors shuffled in and out of boats, chains binding their wrists together as they were scrutinized.

I shake my head, clearing the dark thoughts away. Luckily, this situation is very much different, despite a similar scrutiny, and the girls aren't going to kill me; they need me alive to get brownie points with Clark and somehow boost Amber's chances at president.

The girls shift for me, and Olivia tugs me down so that I'm seated in between her and Leslie, Amber across from us.

The White Bros™ give me looks from the other end of the table, no doubt remembering the whole crime conversation that went down in the juicery the other day. Fortunately for them, that conversation is vaguely replaying in my mind, right next to the Sneaker Store Incident from the weekend.

Eating feels awkward while they're watching me, so I find myself awkwardly glancing between my sandwich and the curious eyes.

Tyler Thompson clears his throat, eyes scouting my untouched BLT sandwich. "So... is that sandwich up for grabs or—?"

To be honest, I can't see myself eating, especially if I'm here for the rest of lunch. I glance up at him, sliding the Ziploc bag to him, with a "sure."

"Hey now," Brett chuckles, and all attention flickers to him, "We don't know where her hands have been."

I'm guessing that comment would've gained scattered laughter had I not been sitting right there. Emory makes eye contact from where he's seated, rubbing his temples.

"Dude, it's in a Ziploc, I'm sure I'll be fine." Tyler replies, laughing as discomfort heats the back of my neck.

Tyler then grimaces, realizing how it sounds. "I mean, I'd eat anything, anyway. Plus," He looks at me this time with a shrug, "I see you sanitize your hands all the time, so..."

It's normally in between classes. Sometimes, I slather some onto my hands during class, just because it's there, hanging off a strap of my backpack.

A nervous tendency.

Eyes flicker to me. I speak up, "Yeah, um, should be fine."

Tyler takes that as an opportunity to rip the sandwich out of the Ziploc, shoveling it into his mouth.

Amber wrinkles her nose, turning to Leslie who decides to change the topic.

"So, the juicery thing was kind of awkward." She says, effectively picking an even worse topic, and increasing the tension at the table.

Amber rolls her eyes. "Let's not talk about that."

"No, no," Brett raises a hand to the air. "No, let's talk about it." His colourless eyes find mine, propping his chin on his hand.

"Tell me more about black-on-black crime."

Maybe it's the exhaustion, maybe it's the tiredness due to Brett's choice to antagonize me, maybe it's remembering the faces of the racists at the shoe shop. Maybe it's sitting down at this table and not being able to feel more out of place... but my energy is completely gone.

"I don't think there's anything more needed to say about it." I finally say, carefully, slowly.

Brett exchanges glances with his friends. "No, seriously, I want to be educated."

The faint smirk on his lips tells me that he doesn't want to be educated, not really. What he *wants* is to press me for information I've already shared, throw around a few scoffs and push me to my breaking point while ignoring the point of every argument.

People like Brett don't want to be *educated*, the very concept is absurd to them, because they've been taught that they're inherently right all their life, so who am I to tell them otherwise?

No one. Absolutely no one.

I'm sure that's what Brett's grandfather, (who I'm sure has ties to the Ku Klux Klan, but I digress), has told him every day since he was born.

"Moving on," Olivia says, noting Amber's annoyance at Brett's resistance to changing the topic.

"Thank you, Olivia," Amber says, leaning forward in her chair. "Anyways, Amina here is pretty good at art. I'm hoping she'd help me with my campaign posters."

My jaw goes slack. This is new.

"I forgot to ask," she asks, pursing her lips,"but would you?"

Leslie nudges me. "We can help you get on Ms. Daniels' good side again."

I was right. Ms. Daniels has a problem with me. She liked me better when I bowed my head, kept my mouth shut. Greatest part of it all is that the entire grade knows it.

"I'm just so preoccupied with schoolwork," I finally say, glancing at her.

"I'll pay for each poster if they reach my expectations," She offers, still noting my hesitance.

I could put money aside, maybe add it to my account for emergency purposes. More importantly, I could write about managing a campaign and being involved in school life in application essays.

College is my way out of the stifling suburbs, it's my ticket out.

Of course I'll be back occasionally, to check in on my parents and Claudie, but I won't ever live in Elkwood again if all goes according to plan.

It also helps that Mrs. Clark is bound to stop giving me a hard time if I'm surrounded by ALO, her treasured girls.

"Okay." I decide, and the grins slide onto the girls' faces while Tyler munches on the BLT, a blank look on his face.

"It's a deal," Amber says, locking eyes with me, a note of finality to her tone.

This should be interesting.

***

When Amber Wesley had said that it was a deal, I hadn't thought that I'd end up back in the juicery, sitting around a table as the three girls work out campaign strategies for Amber.

Maybe I thought that everything would be communicated through text, or they'd backtrack from the whole idea, allowing me to become the not-so-invisible girl again.

They didn't backtrack.

They aren't the most authentic, not the most kind, likely prejudiced, but they stick to an agreement.

Really, it feels like more of a collaboration. More like I'm a contractor, offering my services to ALO so that we can aim for the big goal of getting Amber into StuCo for the coming election.

"I'm thinking something like this," Amber shows me a picture on her phone. "This palette," She swipes through shades of blues and greens, "or this one," She swipes through pinks and burgundys.

I nod.

"I'll send them to you, along with the slogans I want on the posters." She shifts the phone away, and greenish eyes are finally revealed to me.

"Okay," I say, slipping my phone out of my pockets and onto my laps.

"We just need a wow-factor on Amber's posters," Olivia says, waving both hands in the air.

"Then we'll send the money and everything else will follow. You know the drill." Leslie adds, before swiping through her phone and showing something to Amber who giggles.

I purse my lips, my fingers drumming on my laps.

Amber catches my eye, glancing up from Leslie's phone as the two other girls start making teasing comments, something about how Millie's clothes didn't fit right in her post, or how John is all over way too many girls' pages. Their conversation drifts back to Millie's post in an instant.

Amber grabs Leslie's phone from her with a cackle, while typing aloud. "*Ugly as hell.*"

"No," Leslie grabs her phone back, fingers flying across the keyboard. "*Those stretch marks are actually nauseating.*"

"Okay," Olivia giggles. "Tell her to lay off the deep fried Oreos."

Cackles break out from their voices as they type the message, Olivia's hand covering her mouth. Something gross curls up in my stomach, as Amber catches my gaze.

"You can..." She nods towards the exit, and I'm more than ready to head out. My time here is done, and everyone in the space is aware of the fact. I rise to my feet, slinging my backpack over my shoulders.

Nausea builds up in my stomach.

“Bye,” Olivia says, wiggling her fingers before the three of them go back to hovering over Leslie’s phone.

I push through the exit doors, heading onto the sidewalk when I hear my name.

Again.

I have no idea what’s going on today.

My eyes dart in the direction it came from, and it’s Yasmine, dressed in the standard Elkwood vest with a long sleeved shirt underneath, the kilt with leggings beneath, and a grin that rivals the moon.

I give her a smile, and she speeds up to me,

“This is my route home,” She says, falling into step with me.

“Same, I just go around the corner up ahead.” I reply, in an easier tone than I’m used to speaking in. Words seem to come with ease.

“Cool,” She nods, squinting into the distance, raising a hand to shade her face from the bright glare of the sun.

“I thought what you did at the juicery was pretty cool,” I say, uncharacteristically continuing the conversation.

She waves a dismissive hand, a smile rising to her lips. "Dishing out facts is my favorite pastime here." She tucks a black wave behind her ear. "Plus, I usually don't say anything when I do hear them saying ignorant things to you." She pulls her mouth into a line. "And I apologize for that."

"You don't need to apologize," I say, lips pursing.

"Well," She starts, fingers gliding over the golden chain around her neck. "I hold myself to a higher standard than that, unfortunately." A laugh. "I know how it feels to hear people say things like that, so it doesn't look great if I turn a blind eye when it happens to others."

My mouth forms a small 'o', but I don't say anything more as our sneakers tap along the grey pavement, and wind rustles through the trees.

"It's rough," I say, clutching the straps of my backpack, letting out a dry laugh. This town is rough, this school is rough. It's been so incredibly *rough*, lately.

"Agreed," Yasmine nods, and we come to a stop as we reach the intersection.

Her eyes widen as if she remembers something. “You were sitting with Amber, Leslie, and Olivia?”

“Yeah, it’s...” I glance up at the sky, painted in a palette of blues, “A collaboration of some type, I guess.”

“How is it?” She asks, an amused look appearing on her face, tracing her features, her raised eyebrows.

“I honestly don't know. Not great, but not terrible, so that’s something.” I finally say.

“If you’re not sitting with them tomorrow, maybe you could sit with us.” She proposes with a shrug.

I think of the table she shares with the Gamers and the Asians. I could sit with them and Yasmine seems keen on it, I guess. That being said, I don’t interact with members of that table all so often. I bring my bottom lip beneath my teeth.

I’m not sure what to expect.

“It’s fine if you’re not up for it.” Yasmine says, “Just...” She purses her lips. “Let’s see.”

“Alright,” I nod, glancing in the direction of my house.

"Well," Yasmine nods, glancing in the same direction. "Looks like this is where we part."

"Yeah," I wave a hand, letting a tender smile slide to my lips, "See you."

She gives me a military-style salute. "Bye."

Then she's off, heading off in the direction of her own house, and after a few moments, I whip around, heading in the direction of the white villa, something inside me almost wishing I could walk with her for just a little bit longer.

the word

Sitting in the local library, flat on my stomach, I brush strokes of paint across Amber's poster. All my art supplies are spread across the carpeted floor. Bottles of paint, watercolor and acrylic alike. My phone's placed next to me, Amber's palette's staring back up at me through the screen.

There's a signature corner where I do my art. In the crevasse between two bookshelves, at the furthest end of the library, unseen to anyone who walks in. It's the place where I can do my work and my art unbothered; separated from the rest of the world.

My earbuds are still in, and music fills my ears as I quietly nod my head every so often, making sure to keep my strokes steady against the poster board.

"That looks lovely."

My head shoots up to see the librarian, Ms. Knox, standing in front of me, hovering over my poster, a smile tugging at her lips.

I pull my earbuds out of my ear, glancing between the poster and the librarian.

"Thank you," A small smile floats to my lips.

Ms. Knox is one of the few people in this town that I resonate with on such a deep level. She has an aura that I gravitate to. Simple, calm, invested in fictional worlds.

She's three-quarters white, and I doubt anyone except the few black people that live in this town actually know that. She has a mess of curls, constantly pulled into a bun, rounded glasses that stay perched on the edge of her nose, and a toothy smile that's hard to not return.

The first time I met her, crawled up in this exact corner some years ago, I'd known she was black. However, the fact didn't garner much of my attention, as I'd been too busy hiding out in that corner away from the world. My older brother, Nat, had already left for college, meaning I couldn't walk home with him by my side, the iconic brother and sister duo that everyone needed. He was busy most days after school for extracurriculars, but walking home with him always felt safer. More protected.

Although, the week before, he had left for college. I was alone. I had no one to talk to about the everyday crap I'd had to go through, and the specific hatred that I'd faced at school that particular day felt thousands of times worse than any other day.

Then Ms. Knox showed up.

And in that soft voice of hers, she'd sat down next to me, voice comforting as I cried.

She'd told me her own experiences. Told me about the family she grew up in, divided by race and class. Told me about things as light as her favorite colour. Teal. Told me stories of everything.

The library became a safe haven from the rampant storm around me. Ms. Knox became a safe haven.

Ms. Knox grins again, pulling me out of my reverie.

She squints at the page. "Amber, huh?"

I glance back at it to see the name written in all caps, bubbly and visually stunning.

"Yeah, Amber Wesley," I say, as she stoops down next to me, taking in the poster at a closer look.

"Amber's a popular girl, right?" Ms. Knox asks, glancing at me.

I let out a laugh. "I guess you could say that."

"You're making posters for her?" Ms. Knox asks, knitting her eyebrows together.

"She's paying me for it. Apparently she thinks I can make some good art."

Ms. Knox laughs melodically. "Obviously."

I let one shoulder fall into a shrug as a faint grin appears on my lips.

"Taking your braids out any time soon?" Ms. Knox asks, gesturing towards the dark braids that make their way down to my forearms.

"I guess so," I reply, "It's just hard to find people who can do it, and Mom doesn't have all the time in the world."

Ms. Knox nods.

"I'll probably have to wear it out... it's just..." I trail off, nightmares of the students touching and messing around with my hair crashing down on me like a ton of bricks.

"They're going to treat me like some exotic animal, and don't even get me started on the type of comments Brett's going to make." I mutter, rubbing my temples.

Ms. Knox rubs a circle onto my back. "You're too young to be stressed. If anyone tries anything, report it."

I give her a look. "When has reporting ever done anything in Elkwood?" I don't add, *for me,* but I know that she hears it.

She sighs. "I can't imagine the joys of being the only black girl in the entire school." Ms. Knox says, raising a hand to her forehead, and pretending to swoon at the romanticness of the whole situation.

"Oh, the joys are endless, Ms. Knox." I repeat in a bougie accent, holding a hand to my chest and letting sarcasm drip from my tone.

Our eyes meet, and soon, laughter escapes both of our lips, filling the little cranny for a few moments.

"How about coffee?" Ms. Knox finally says, rising to her feet, as I rise to mine as well.

"I don't drink coffee when it's not Monday," I reply, still smiling as I shove my things into my backpack, hanging the poster on a window to dry.

Coffee is a necessity to get through Mondays. However, I actually want to get some sleep throughout the rest of the week and *not* have my heart pounding at 100 beats per minute.

"Right," Ms. Knox says, lips twitching. "I always forget that you're a hot cocoa addict."

Then we're off, teases filling the air as we head out of the library and to the coffee place next door.

***

The cafe is warm, the smell of coffee beans filling the entire space. It's almost been a ritual between Ms. Knox and I ever since we first met years ago.

I clasp my mug of hot chocolate, allowing it to warm my hands as Ms. Knox speaks to me about new visitors to the libraries and reads that she highly recommends.

Our conversation is light, and a few minutes later, Ms. Knox and I are rising from our seats, Ms. Knox paying for our drinks despite my usual protests.

The chime jingles on our way out of the door, me holding the door open and allowing Ms. Knox to walk through before following behind her.

"Thanks for the hot chocolate, Ms. Knox," I say, a half smile rising to my face as the warmth from the hot chocolate settles in my chest.

Ms. Knox waves a hand. "This is our ritual, isn't it?"

"I guess," I say, as we make our way down the sidewalk, towards the library.

My eyes drift over to the side, and leaning against the wall is a man. He's hunched over, skin rough and dirty, calloused hands linked over his frayed jeans. His grey eyes stay on us, not much of a contrast to his pale skin.

I almost want to stop. He seems like he doesn't have a home, but he might just be under the influence, something that his bloodshot eyes indicate. He opens his mouth in a sneer, scarce teeth being revealed.

I tell myself to walk faster, but my legs refuse to cooperate. Noticing my halt, Ms. Knox slows down, still several feet in front of me. Her eyes drift over to the man leaning against the wall, and she gives me a nearly imperceptible jut of her chin, an indication to keep walking.

The man's eyes meet mine. Cold and unwavering. He smiles. Not a nice smile and not a friendly smile. This is a leer more than anything. It twists his lips into a sinister grin.

I step back, discomfort curling at my insides, anxiety steadily rising as he meets my eyes, cigarette held between his fingers.

Then, "What're you looking at?"

I don't respond, breaths coming in and out, quicker and quicker.

"Hey," He drawls. "I'm talking to you!"

I beg the universe to leave me alone. Just this once. And isn't it *just my luck* that he's staring right at me. A shaky breath slips from my lips and into the cool air. Not today. *Please* not today.

My feet move faster.

Then a cough, a scuff of a cigarette, a raspy scoff.

Then he says it, the word.

My heart stops.

Everything seems to slow down infinitely. The rest of the world becomes a blur of nothing. Life freezes into ice.

The first time I remember being called that word, I was five. I was spinning around in a floral dress on the wide expanse of field near our house in the city my family used to live in.

There were white men on the field, all decked out in t-shirts and shorts, playing an impromptu game of football. And as I was running by, my Dad laughing as he followed after me, they watched us.

Their game hadn't started yet, so Dad was following me off the side of the field, guiding me towards the exit so they'd have the full expanse of field, despite them only needing about half of it. There were flowers, one in my hair that Dad had put there, and I was spinning and singing as the end of the field came closer.

And it was then that one of the men sporting the cold, watching eyes had spoken up. His head was shaved, eyes pale, lips pulled into a dark scowl. Unprecedented anger curled up his face, and in moments he was yelling. Profanities and other things. But the thing that I remember vividly was him turning in the direction of my Dad, many feet away as he yelled, *"get that [slur] girl off the field!"*

I had never seen someone so angry before, and for no apparent reason. I stopped spinning, stopped moving. Dad shook his head, exhaled. There was a tug of war in his eyes as his shoulders sagged and he lifted me up onto his shoulders, proposing that we get some ice-cream later as we left the field.

Now, I feel the exact same punch I felt that day, back when I didn't even know what the word meant, but knew it was meant to cut right through my soul.

My breaths come in and out, quicker and quicker and quicker. I can't stop them as my chest heaves violently.

My heartbeat skips, trips over itself, stutters, pounds harder and harder and harder.

My gaze falls to trembling hands as my body shakes, and I can't stop it.

I can't stop it.

Don't let it get to you. I hear my mind say. *Don't let him see you cry.*

Everything cuts through my mind in flashes. Shackles. Someone pushed to the ground. Someone set on fire, hung, violated in every aspect of their humanity.

The last word my predecessors heard before their life was wrenched from their blooming chests.

The man's smile never drops.

The word tears right through me, and familiar spots cloud my vision. *Not again.*

Ms. Knox grabs my wrist, tethering me back to the world. She turns to the man in a way I know my mom would never be able to afford to as someone who doesn't pass, "that is disgusting." Every word is cuttingly emphasized from her lips.

The man laughs.

Ms. Knox tugs me away. I trip over my steps, the world becoming a hazy blur.

I vaguely see the man pick something from the floor. A newspaper of some sort. He flips through it, going about his life. Because that's just another day in life to him. Meanwhile, the incident will plague my nightmares for years.

It's a word that I can't even utter when music fills my universe. A word I push to the back of my mind. A word that I want to be eradicated.

Ms. Knox sits me down in the library.

I curl in on myself, arms clutching my legs, legs pulled to my chest.

"Sweetheart," Ms. Knox must be saying.

I can't hear anything. Not a word. Chills. I feel a cold rush through my body.

Sobs. I'm sobbing.

I rock back and forth. Back and forth. My face is damp, but I don't know how.

"I called your parents,." I hear again.

I still rock back and forth, my lips quiver.

I slow down.

"Breathe."

I *can't*. I can't find my breath. I struggle to even inhale, because my chest won't allow it. *Breathe*. My breaths come out shaky.

"You can get through this." Her voice is gentle, trusting. Comfort rings through it.

"Is there anything you need?" She asks.

My eyes glazed, I shake my head.

"Focus on your breathing," She says. I count with her up to ten, my rocking slows, I release shaky breaths. Her figure comes into view.

Last exhale. My entire body sags. Ms. Knox rests her hands on my shoulders, then after a beat, pulls my fragile body onto hers, rubbing my back.

***

I barely say a word for the rest of the afternoon. Ms. Knox hovers near me, and I let myself draw strokes along the poster. I don't think about it.

I drink water.

My parents arrive minutes later.

They rub my back, give me reassuring smiles and soft words. Maybe I nod.

They talk to Ms. Knox, standing off to the side, hushed voices, gazes drifting towards me every few moments.

"*Panic attack,*" Is what I hear them say.

However, I barely register it, just keep working on Amber's poster.

By the time I'm done, there are beautiful strokes of blues that mirror the sky. AMBER is spelled at the top in all capitals. Her slogan is positioned right above the bottom, all in cerulean cursive. A circle is smack in the middle of a poster, empty for a picture of Amber to be placed.

I don't smile as I scope my work, my eyes roving over the board, but I think Amber's poster looks beautiful.

And it poses a welcome distraction from the sweat trickling down my spine, or the words echoing in my mind.

Amber's poster is beautiful. Everything's fine.

I wonder how many times I'll have to repeat that before I believe it.

Everything's fine. *Everything's perfect*, I assure the universe.

Hail hits at the glass windows from outside. My bottom lip trembles as lightning slices through the dark sky.

The universe doesn't seem to believe me either.

art supplies

Moving is a strange concept.

Not just strange, but otherworldly. It sounds like a strange concept in theory, because moving means that my entire world will change or morph into something different.

And would that necessarily be a bad thing?

After the sneaker incident, the juicery debate, and the n-word debacle, moving doesn't sound like the worst idea right now.

I peer over the shelves, eyes glazing over bottles of paints, fingers finding poster boards and stickers.

I'd been hesitant to accept Amber's invitation to the art shop today for those reasons.

It honestly seems like wherever I go, something bad is bound to happen. I was looking for sneakers. *Literal* sneakers, and then I had someone follow me throughout the store. I'd been trying to get juice for Claudie when Brett decided to bring black on black crime into a conversation. I'd been walking to the library from the cafe when some old white man decided he was going to call me the n-word just because he felt like it.

But what would I say to Amber? *Can't. I've recently had a flurry of racist interactions that have been extremely detrimental to my mental health, so I'm gonna have to pass on this one.*

Something in me kind of wanted to go to the art store, anyway. Plus, with Amber right next to me, I almost have a shield of some sort.

"This one's gorgeous." Amber says, and my eyes drift from the shelves to her.

She's holding a pastel blue background with white swirls of clouds touching the blue. She purses her lips, slipping another one from the shelf.

"This one?" She asks, holding it up.

It's a bright poster background, abstract with a variety of different shapes, all overlapping in different colours.

"It stands out," I decide. Amber glances at it briefly, tossing it into a basket.

"You have enough paint, right?" She asks, making her way through the aisle.

"Yeah," I reply, following after her. "I think I do."

"*This*," She whips around to face me, shaking a bottle of silver glitter in my face, before tossing it into the basket.

"Too much of it'll be tacky, but you'll make it work, right?" She asks, then laughs. "Well, that's what I'm paying you for, anyway."

"I can make it work," I say, analyzing the contents of the basket.

"My campaign is going to be great," Amber decides, hands resting on the hips of her high-waisted jeans.

"No one's going to stop me from winning this thing," She says, tucking a strand of hair behind her ear and scanning the rest of the shop.

"I mean," She says, walking faster and beckoning for me to come along with her, "The only person running against me is Walter, and well," She lets out an amused, matter-of-factly laugh, giving me a knowing look. "You know."

Something flares in my chest, slight but there.

Walter Cohen doesn't really stand a chance against Amber. Not with the huge glasses that seem to dwarf his face, or the skinny limbs that give the impression that he's a walking twig. He's one of those kids who gives the impression that they know a lot more than you do, or that you can't even begin to grasp the multitude of intelligence that supposedly resides in his brain.

Sure, other kids like Brett or Amber have the exact same attitude, but the difference is that they're supposed to be attractive, meaning that they could run over people with trucks and they'd be thanked for it.

I'm sure Amber could wear the exact same glasses Walt wears, but would be called cute and chic for it. She can talk down to other people the same way Walt does without them batting an eye. Whereas if Walt does that, he'll get beat up by the White Bros™ or scoffed at by the general student population.

It probably doesn't help that everyone in this town seems to be ignorant about conditions and Walt has ADHD. While it isn't his fault, it doesn't stop him from getting singled out or prevent people from giving him a hard time, what with the way blank looks and the r-slur travels through the hallway more often than not.

Aside from ADHD, though, Walt *can* be kind of a prig, still unnecessarily salty just like anyone else at Elkwood, sometimes more so.

Despite the fact that Walt isn't the nicest person nor the easiest to get along with, something in me bristles at the way Amber talks about him, at the smugness dripping from her tone like he never had a chance.

I purse my lips, letting my shoulders sag.

"Anyways," Amber says, "I think that's enough. Let's go."

So, we make our way up to the front counter, placing all the supplies on the front desk, Amber grabbing one of those fuzzy pens and adding it to the pile.

People's eyes only drift to us for a second before drifting back to their phones or over-active toddlers. I'm next to Amber, and there's almost a: *don't worry, she's with me* attitude that radiates from the two of us together. It's the first time I've ever had a shield outside of my house, the white villa. Amber takes the receipts, and we each hold a bag as we leave the store. Not unlike the white villa, she's the shield, the castle wall, the moat that's deterring the racists.

I don't know how to feel about that.

So, I don't bother feeling.

Amber hands me the rest of the art supplies, shoving them into my hands, while she holds her phone to her ear, calling someone to pick her up.

"Alright," She says, hanging up. "Campaign week is in one and a half weeks," Her gaze drifts to the supplies. "Have the posters done by next week, and we should be fine."

"Cool," I say. There's an awkward few moments of silence.

"Okay. Do you, like, have a car?" Amber finally asks, eyebrows raised as though that's a required question to ask, a burden for her to ask.

"Oh, my house isn't too far from here." Pause. "My bike's over there." I say, nodding towards the pale blue bicycle that's leaning against the red brick wall.

She nods. "Okay." Pause. She purses her lips, scrolls through her phone as she says it, signalling the end of our conversation.

A rowdy car pulls in, ridiculously loud music pumping, teenage boys and a few girls sticking their heads out of the windows. Tyler's messy blonde head pokes out of the window as he whoots.

Amber makes her way into the car, not looking back once. I purse my lips as she slides into shotgun, and the car sloppily pulls out of the driveway.

With that, I slide onto my bicycle and peddle down the sidewalk, not bothering to look back as my braids fly behind me.

***

When lunch arrives the next school day, I actually end up taking Yasmine's offer.

Not like I had much competition either way. As of now, I have three options: sit by myself, sit with her, or sit with ALO and the

White Bros™ while Brett visually cuts daggers into me and makes some accidentally-on-purpose racist jokes.

I don't necessarily approach the table, seeing as I'm not bold like that, but I see Yasmine in the lunch line, and she ends up walking me to the direction of her table.

She slides onto her table, patting the seat next to her, where I sit down.

Some of the kids look up from their conversations, casually glancing at me, and the gamers don't remove their gazes from their devices, two of them talking about something on Reddit.

"Brought someone over," Yasmine says, smoothing down her forehead, and glancing about the table.

Jennifer Zhang raises up a hand in a barely-there wave while giving me a nod. I always wonder how Jennifer strikes the balance between being a "good girl" and a "bad girl".

Her grades are decent, she's not smarter than she lets on, but she's witty in an almost natural way, as if it's a way of life for her. She's calm, but not docile. I'm guessing if you mess around with her, she can teach you a thing or two.

We don't come across each other all that much, though. So, all my observations are just that; observations.

Jennifer's eyes return to her phone.

The rest of the people at the table are okay, but distant. Some of the smiles touching their lips seem less genuine, more forced. Some don't look up. Others smile a little before returning back to conversation.

Yasmine's the one that keeps a conversation with me going, grinning at me like I'm supposed to be here and not like I'm supposed to feel as awkward as I do.

A conversation arises to the air from a few seats away from me, and I distractedly tune in, the clattering of the cafeteria a melody in the background.

"See, I don't know whether or not I'll even get into an Ivy League because spots are being given to random students off the streets." He lowers his voice, leaning forward. "Just because they're..." A pause, as his voice drops to a whisper, "African American."

It's Kevin. Kevin Choi. An award-winning smile, and a decent tennis player. Also, however, an intense know-it-all with the grades to boot.

Kevin runs a hand through black hair, raising both hands as he talks to one of his friends who are seated across from him, voice quieting. "And no offense to them, okay, but I didn't put all this work into schoolwork to be shorthanded and have my spot stolen."

Stolen.

Yasmine blinks, meets my eyes, blinks again. Her expression seems painful. She smiles a little weakly, shaking her head as the two boys converse.

"Nah, that's completely fair." It's one of Kevin's friends. He has one of those rounded glasses that fall down the slope of his nose time and time again. "I have a solid 4.0 GPA and like hell I'm going to let someone take my hard-earned work away from me." A pause. "Like, you're not *that* oppressed. The past might've been rough. Thing is, you can't put *me* at a disadvantage because of that."

The topic, of course, is affirmative action. A wry grin curves onto my lips. *I chose the best day to sit at Yasmine's table, didn't I?* My smile falters when it dawns on me that this may in fact be an everyday conversation starter.

The two boys continue, sharing stories, maybe along the lines of their parents coming to this country with hope, with nothing, and despite that fact, their parents succeeded even with life's obstacles. That if their parents could do that, why couldn't everyone else's?

I don't feel up to telling Kevin Choi that my ancestors fought hard for their ability to have rights in this country. Despite barely having rights themselves. We fought for each other.

I don't tell him that Asian American and Pacific Islander presence has actually increased in colleges in recent years.

I don't feel up to telling him that my ancestors were barred from schools—something that was backed up by the law— and weren't allowed to read, were tied to train tracks if they were the slightest bit knowledgeable.

I don't tell him that the American Dream doesn't exist. Slaves worked hard *plenty* but received nothing in return for their labor.

I certainly don't tell him that I have a higher GPA than him, a 4.15 in actuality. I won't ever be stealing a spot, I'll be earning it.

Instead, I smile wanly, try to slow my speedening heart rate.

I wonder why Kevin Choi needs to make this a competition. Needs to make this an *us* vs. *them*.

The answer resides behind my chest.

Society. Tensions. The model minority rhetoric. The reasons why all the people of color at this school aren't holding hands and singing Kumbaya together.

Division, history, the narrative.

Maybe, one day, I'll be able to tell him all of this. Maybe, one day, we'll talk, instead of avoiding glances in the halls, instead of having a chasm between us.

Today is not that day.

I exhale, eyes fluttering shut.

"Hey." Yasmine cuts into my thoughts like a razor-blade. The boys glance over at me at that, eyes slightly widening and voices hushing as they avert their gazes.

Yasmine clears her throat, tossing a bag of skittles over to me, and we purse our lips as we divide the skittles, trying to colour-code them. It's nice, laughing with someone like this.

My thoughts carefully float away from Kevin's conversation, and I let myself breathe for a few seconds, because all I want to do is fall away from this seemingly endless battle that I have with the world.

The moment's calming, and I can practically hear the mellow, dainty music playing in the background.

That's until someone pokes me in my shoulder roughly.

Cue the record scratch.

I look up to see the one and only ALO. Now, *that* appearance is what catches the attention of everyone at the table. The gamers look up, and so do the other Asian kids seated around the table, conversations halting. Jennifer glances up from her phone.

"Hey, guys." Leslie says, eyes scouting the kids seated at the table, boredom faintly touching her irises, "Vote Amber for president."

Amber curtsies, ever the politician, while their eyes stay on her, some shrugging at the request.

"We need to borrow Amina for a bit," Olivia takes my wrist, pulling me to my feet. Yasmine raises both eyebrows and I return the look.

We make our way to the far end of the cafeteria, next to the microwaves.

"What was that, Amina?" Amber snaps.

I knit my eyebrows together. "I'm hanging out with Yasmine and her friends?"

"We can see that," Leslie says, eyebrow arched.

"Alright, then what's up?" I ask, head slightly tilted in question. " If you're worried about the posters, don't be. I'm working on them."

"It's not about the posters," Olivia says, leaning back against the wall.

Amber briefly glances in the direction of Yasmine's table.

"First of all, sitting over there?" She juts a thumb at the table. "Bad move." She says, shaking her head. "This is actually terrible for my campaign."

"You literally got their votes," I say, and can faintly hear the slight irritation creeping into my tone.

"No, I *literally* did not," Amber said, "They're Walt's friends. Yeah, some of them will vote for me, but a lot of them have an insane urge to topple the social hierarchy." She glances up at the ceiling before gesturing towards the drama kids.

"Like them. They think they're insanely edgy and above all of this." She chuckles in a way that seems more salty than anything. "They aren't."

"It's not that big of a deal," I say, laughing lightly. My laugh is a feather, but the strain behind it is concrete.

"Oh my God, Amina. It's not about a personal vendetta or something petty like that," Leslie chips in, rolling her eyes and shaking her head, letting the single braid swing back and forth.

"This is politics," Olivia says, pursing her lips, "It's about strategy."

"Exactly," Amber says, "Sorry to be blunt, but I don't know if you've noticed that these aren't the most popular kids in the school."

I raise my eyebrows.

"It's not about them, personally. It's about the rest of Elkwood. People were watching you sit down with them. Most of them won't think twice about it until the elections arrive." She pauses. "It's already a huge risk to be taking you into our campaign. If we play our cards right, it could be a huge win."

My eyebrows fly higher, and I let out a dry laugh, shaking my head.

Amber plows on. "People see you hanging out with them, they associate it with me. If you're helping me out with my campaign, you have to represent me well."

"If you mess up, it reflects on Amber," Leslie says. "Brett already hates Abadi or what's-her-face—"

"—*Yasmine*," I say.

"Whatever. He's never liked her, but when she butted herself into the conversation at the juicery, he started to dislike her a hell of a lot more."

I give her a look.

"It's like a close friend of the president hanging around a former KKK member." Olivia explains.

My eyebrows fly upwards at the comparison."I'm sorry, are you comparing the KKK to Yasmine and her friends?" I ask, mouth parted.

"*Simile*, honey," Leslie says. "This is just how it works here."

Analogy, I think, *and a hyperbole.*

"You hang around with the wrong people, your friends get that name, too. You hang out with certain people," Amber gestures towards the table before gesturing towards herself, "you mess up your friend's campaign for president."

"We're all friends, right?" Olivia asks, leaning forward.

"Sure." The words feel uncertain on my lips, as though I am trying them out but they don't sit right.

"Then, once Amber's campaign is over and she's won, you can hang out with them all you want." Leslie says, lazily gesturing towards Yasmine's table.

"Listen, sit with Abadi again and Brett won't support my campaign. None of his friends will, either." Amber emphasizes. He's influential, and we're all well-aware of the fact, but Amber refuses to say it. "We don't need a divide between our friends at the table," Amber says, gesturing towards the table where the White Bros™ are seated.

What it looks like is Amber realizing that her and Brett's popularity levels are too close for comfort. Even though she'd never admit it, I'm certain Amber knows that Brett isn't the nicest guy. So, she's wary. *Why?* She knows that Brett would mess with her campaign for a reason as petty as her association with people he dislikes. Especially someone who had crossed him earlier.

Olivia gives me a meaningful look, and I'm already catching onto the main ideas. Firstly, Brett's extremely petty, and due to that pettiness, the guy could ruin Amber's campaign in seconds.

I almost want to ask, *"If Brett's really your friend, why would he mess around with your campaign?"*

However, I don't ask.

Instead, I just let them give me faux smiles, Olivia patting my shoulder gently before they all sidle past me and return to their table.

Yasmine looks up from where she's seated, mouthing a: *what was that?*

I'm not necessarily sure what to say, because the entire conversation is still flying through my mind. So, when Yasmine meets my eyes, her own eyes inquisitive, I can only shrug in response.

laura johnson

There's a new girl.

When new people come to Elkwood, they're always scrutinized, always observed, casually taken in. Within a week, tops, they'll find out where they fit on the social ladder.

They might stray towards the Ambiguous Whites, maybe the Asians and Gamers, the drama kids, or if they end up hitting the jackpot—to most people, at least— they'll end up sitting with ALO and the White Bros™.

My first glance at the new girl tells me that she can't really fit into any of these groups, which is absolutely abnormal. In fact, before I saw the new girl, I heard about her.

Amber had come by my locker earlier today, all chirpy and trying not to act like just two days ago, she'd tried to dictate who I sat with just so that she could stay in Brett's good books and win the StuCo elections.

I'm not impressed, but that doesn't mean I didn't listen to her. We had something resembling a deal, after all, and I guess I'm not planning on breaking it.

Rewinding to earlier this morning, Amber had leaned in close, asking, "*have you seen the new girl?*"

Then, at that point, Leslie had popped out of nowhere like some cursed apparition, hissing, "I think she's Indian."

I had half a mind to ask if she was referring to actual Indians from South Asia, or if the sky had fallen, and there was actually a Native American at Elkwood.

However, I stopped myself *real quick*, because I know my townspeople are highly unlikely to be referring to a South Asian. Also, I'm not all that convinced that Leslie's capable of pointing out the country of India on a map, either way.

Had I gone ahead and asked: *"Do you mean a Native American? An Indigenous person? The first people to tread this land?"* I'm sure Leslie would've rolled her eyes and muttered something borderline racist, that I would've decidedly chosen to ignore.

I'd known then—with the frenzy illustrated on their faces—that the new girl wasn't a white-passing or ambiguous Native American, this was someone who was clearly non-white, and therefore went startlingly uncategorized in the Elkwood status quo.

Now that I'm glancing at the new girl, I see long black hair falling down to her waist, the pretentious Elkwood uniform hanging from her slender body, olive skin bright and unabashed, and eyes scouting the area with something resembling skepticality.

A curious grin curves onto my lips. Really, I should say something, talk to her.

Not that I would, though. However, something curls at my insides when I realize that she—just like me— doesn't necessarily have a group of people like her in Elkwood, no one she can identify with. I hate that, because all of a sudden, I see myself from a few years ago, walking through these hallways, being the odd one out. Being the only person like me.

The warning bell rings, and the new girl turns a corner, long hair swishing as she enters a classroom. I let out a breath, turning towards my own classroom, intensely resisting the urge to look back.

***

The new girl continues to be a topic for the next two classes. People don't make an extremely huge deal out of her presence, but the whole buzz surrounding her presence is unnecessary. Thing is, at Elkwood, you don't want people talking about you. It rarely ever means something positive.

Second period comes, and class starts, everyone seated, eyes flickering to somewhere in the room. I glance in the direction of their gazes, and sure enough, the new girl sits there, hands clasped over her desk, eyes on the teacher instead of the dozens of students watching her.

"We have a new student," Ms. Wilson smiles, beckoning for the new girl to rise to her feet. "Introduce yourself to the class."

"Laura," She says, hands tapping at her sides.

"One interesting thing about yourself?" Ms. Wilson asks.

"I was on the swim team in my old school," Laura says with a shrug.

"Very nice," Ms. Wilson says, ushering her back to her seat. "Unfortunately, we don't have a swim team here." She shrugs, letting out a little laugh while adjusting her floral blouse.

Laura purses her lips before giving a half smile, "That's too bad."

"Indeed," Ms. Wilson says blandly before returning to today's topic for history class.

"Well, time to go over the Post-Classical Era," Ms. Wilson says, clapping her hands together as some members of the class let out quiet groans.

***

The bell rings, signalling that history class is over. As usual, the whole class was uncomfortable to sit through, and Brett was adding his unnecessary input throughout the entire period. Not to mention that my history was completely absent from today's class. So, essentially, history class today wasn't anything abnormal.

I shuffle all my supplies into my backpack, slinging it over my shoulders in one smooth motion. Soon, I'm down the hall, opening my locker, only to be greeted by a multitude of books hurtling down at me.

They clatter to the ground, making the surrounding students glance towards me, some raising their hands to their mouths to conceal laughter.

I shouldn't have stuffed everything in my locker last time.

Clearly, my one brain cell might not be functioning the way it should.

With this in mind, I stoop down to the ground, clearing my supplies from the floor, a string of curses flying through my mind. That is, until a hand scrapes some stray pens from the floor, holding them out to me.

My mouth parts. Not in Elkwood. Whenever my things fall to the ground, people'll ignore it, and if they're feeling *real* generous, they'll kick it away, out of my reach. Helping out? They've never heard of her.

So, who the hell is actually helping me out?

My eyes drift upwards, and there she is. Laura. Her mouth is drawn into a casual line, and I take the pens out of her hands, with a "*thank you.*"

"Yeah, it's fine," She glances about, catching the eyes of the surrounding students. "It didn't look like anyone else was about to help."

Welcome to Elkwood, I think, dryly.

I purse my lips, rising to my feet with my supplies in hand. "Kids here are more... independent."

A slightly raised eyebrow hints that Laura doesn't buy my halfhearted excuse, either.

"Or," She says as I stuff my supplies in my locker and remove my lunch bag from it, "they just have crap personalities."

I crack a smile at that. “Or that,” I agree, in a much quieter tone as Laura lets out a laugh.

Her eyes meet mine. “Laura.”

Maintaining her gaze, I exhale my name. “Amina.” She nods at that as I sling my backpack over my shoulder.

Laura waits for a couple of moments, and I find myself falling into step with her, heading in the direction of the cafeteria.

“They were staring at me like I’d grown a third head,” Laura says in a lower tone.

“Like you didn’t belong here,” I say, almost automatically. After all, I’m not unfamiliar with those expressions.

Laura glances over at me, curiously, with a nod, as we enter the cafeteria. I pass by ALO’s table, instead, heading over to my singular table.

“Ironic,” Laura says, smoothly, as we slide into seats across from each other.

I exhale a soft laugh, ignoring the eyes that turn towards us. That one word just about sums it up.

She pulls out a sandwich, a self-satisfied grin curving onto her lips.

I can practically feel Amber's glare burning through my flesh from the other side of the cafeteria. I don't turn around. Laura lets herself lean back in her seat while she eats, and I have to respect her easy, self-assured demeanor, the way she didn't hesitate sitting with me on her first day.

"You're fine here?" I ask, glancing over at Yasmine who seems to be in deep conversation with Jennifer and one of the gamers. I glance back at Laura.

"I'd hope so," Laura says, dryly.

"No, I mean, sitting next to me will probably destroy any chance you have of *not* being othered. Essentially social suicide." I amend.

Laura purses her lips, scanning the cafeteria, before turning to me, deadpanning. "I think I'll live if these people don't like me."

A half smile curves onto my lips.

"So, I saw some posters around here," She says, pursing her lips. "Stu-Co elections?" She asks.

"Oh, yeah." I say, thinking of Amber's posters. "Seems like this year's elections are going to be uneventful, though."

Laura hums, tucking a dark strand behind her ear. "I've seen Stu-Co elections at my old school. Maybe I'll sign up," She says, with a shrug.

Before I can reply, a pale hand slaps the table, drawing our attention to the owner of it. I'm just about ready to say something to Amber when I see that it isn't Amber, but Brett.

He sits a few seats away from us, manspreading in his typical fashion. "So... you," He says, turning to Laura, the entire comfort at the table vanishing into thin air.

"Yeah?" Laura replies, glancing at me, briefly.

"You're new here. Why'd you move?" He asks, leaning forward.

"Many reasons," she replies, voice easy as the wind.

There's an awkward few moments of silence, and I poke at my mac and cheese with my fork, eyebrows scrunched together as I analyze Brett.

"Heard you say that you're thinking of running for president," Brett says, breaking into the silence.

Laura raises her eyebrows, voice calm, but eyes suspiciously cutting into Brett. "Yeah, I think I will." Pause. "It's great to try new things, take risks."

There almost seems to be a stare-off, cutting glances being exchanged. Laura's already challenging Brett without saying a word. She's being subtle about it, of course, but she's not cowering. She's resisting.

I realize, with my eyes intense, back straightened and posture firm, I'm deathly close to doing the same thing.

Brett lets out a low laugh. "I'm sure you took plenty of risks at your old school."

Something crosses over Laura's face, and her eyes remain steady on Brett, feet tapping the floor, gently.

Brett taps the table, rising to his feet with a laugh. "Maybe I'll run, too." He smirks. "Like you said, it's good to take risks."

Then he adjusts the collar of his vest, running a hand through his hair as he saunters away from our table.

I'm barely processing what just happened, or the undertones of Brett's snide comment, but Laura returns to her sandwich, eyes suddenly fascinated by the array of windows to our right.

"Running would be a good idea," I say, without a second thought. Laura glances at me and my lips curve up, slightly. "And I mean, if you wanted, I could..." A pause, an exhale. "I could be your campaign manager?"

I blink at my own words. After all, I'm already a campaign manager for Amber. However, with her, I'm stifled; a prop, a tool.

Despite having been able to brush it off earlier in the campaign, something deep inside my chest wants me to be free, something in my chest believes that I'm more than just a tool to be disposed of at the end of the day.

Laura stares at me for a moment, a smirk breaking out onto her lips as she eyes the center table from where we're seated. Her gaze returns to mine and her smirk widens, the shine in her eyes mirroring mine.

"Alright," She says, leaning forward with a sly glint to her eyes, "Let's knock 'em dead."

deal's over

"I'm sorry, you did *what?*" Amber hurries after me, her Mary Janes clacking on the sidewalk beneath our feet as I walk faster.

I let out a breath, "I told you, Amber, I'm helping Laura out with her campaign."

"No, I heard you, and you're supposed to be helping *me* with my campaign." Amber says, face tinged with an angry pink.

"You asked me to help with your campaign posters," I say, a breath escaping my lips. "I did that. I can make more if you want, but that doesn't mean I can't be someone else's campaign manager. I'm your contractor, your poster-designer."

"Okay, what about Mrs. Clark?" Leslie asks, speeding up to the two of us, eyebrow arched.

"Let's be honest here," I start, shrugging distractedly, "Mrs. Clark can't help me with anything at this point. Yeah, you guys could've helped me get on her good side, and that would be great for college reference letters."

I exhale at the cutting feeling in my ribs. That's most definitely a loss.

"Exactly," Olivia cuts in, waving her arms, "She could write you a good letter of recommendation that you wouldn't otherwise have."

"True, but, I can ask someone else," I say, more for my own benefit that anything else, "I'll find someone else."

Leslie lets out an icy laugh. "I doubt that."

"And by the way," Amber says from next to me, "Mrs. Clark *wanted* us to take you in. We're doing you a huge favor, and this is how you pay us back?" She lets out an incredulous scoff. "You should be grateful, Amina. We put a lot on the line just to help you out. We didn't need to do that. We *didn't* need to invite you to sit with us."

I stop in my tracks, now completely done with giving placating replies. A sardonic laugh escapes my lips.

"I'm not your little project," I say, watching Olivia's face pale at the accusation. "I'm not a little chihuahua that you can stuff in your purse." I pause. "I'm not your pet." Leslie raises a finger, but I plow on. "I'm my own person."

I shake my head. "We were working collaboratively, and if anything, Amber, I was doing *you* a favor by helping with your campaign posters for a few dollars." I say, eyes carefully boring into them. "Things have gone too far. I mean, you literally dictated who I could sit with for the face of your campaign."

Leslie rolls her eyes, subtly.

"Not to mention how Brett was acting throughout," I say, fingers drumming at my sides. Implying that I was dirty, bringing up "black-on-black crime" around me at every opportunity he got.

"Alright," Amber says, "I draw a line there. We didn't say any of the things Brett said to you."

I raise my hands in the air. "Well, you sure as hell didn't stop him. I mean, you *laughed*, Amber."

The pinkish tinge to Amber's cheeks become a deep red, and I'm guessing it's not from anger, not anymore.

The baggage in my chest is gone now that I've let everything out, and softness replaces it.

"I guess," I start, slowly, "What I'm trying to say is that you *say* that we're all friends, but you act differently. So, this is where *I* have to draw the line."

"I'm sorry," I say, sliding my fingers through the straps of my backpack. "I'm just not cool with that."

Olivia opens her mouth before it closes again.

“You’re also not the nicest to other people, either.” I say, quietly. “Like, trolling Millie on Instagram? Not a super great look for a presidential candidate.”

Pink rises to Olivia’s cheeks, now matching Amber’s flushed face.

“Anyway, I think I have to leave,” I say with a wry nod. “Good luck on your campaign, Amber.”

With that, I continue on my way, the girls frozen into place as I adjust my backpack and continue to speed walk ahead of them, leaving what feels like weeks of problems behind me.

the whole history debate

My eyes fly open as I stretch across my bed, sunlight filtering into my room, as it painfully dawns on me that today is the day that Ms. Wilson and Mr. Pham are orchestrating the debate.

During history class.

I run a hand through long braids, debating whether or not to peel myself off of the safe haven of my thick mattress and plush blankets.

I don't know if I'm ready to stumble through the rest of this week. I trill my lips. Unfortunately, I've never had much of a choice. With that resigned resolution, I slide off of my bed and into my bathroom, brushing my teeth and rinsing off.

The putting-on of my school uniform has become a natural ritual at this point. So, it's easy for me to smooth down the pale dress shirt, do all the buttons, button my kilt around its waist. It's easy for me to pull on the high socks, making my way to the mirror to adjust the tie.

My eyes find mine. Brown and wide. They drift to my face. Deep, cocoa brown skin that Mom claims glows in the sun, a slightly jutting chin, a gentle slope of my nose, ink-black eyelashes that curl upwards, lips that are pulled into a full line.

Lips that might've used to smile more.

Pursing my lips, my reflection does the same. It was a reflection I used to want to change, scrub off. After all, going to the playground and hearing the insisting: *"You can't play with us,"* or the: *"You can't be* (insert tacky princess here) *because you don't look like her."*

Back then, I *needed* to be Cinderella, Aurora, Snow White. And I *needed* to play with the pink dress-clad girls who better fit the descriptions of these princesses than I ever would. So, I wandered after them, asking to play, being pushed aside.

I blink at my reflection. Exhaling, I step away from the mirror.

Either way, my appearance won't be a factor in the hell-fest of the history debate that is bound to occur today.

The debate is supposed to be less rigid this class. Anyone and everyone can pitch in if they so choose— granted they follow the moderator's guidance.

The tie finally takes shape, and I carefully pull it up to achieve that bougie, preppy look that irritates me and comforts me at the same time.

I'm not even ready to think about how the whole thing will play out. If Brett's constant outbursts in history class are any indication— the whole debate is likely to be chaos.

As a member of the debate team, Mr. Pham has emphasized that we should step up as leaders of the group. We'll see how *that* turns out.

With that in mind, I stumble down the stairs, grabbing some toast, smearing some butter onto it and popping it into my mouth. Then, I'm rushing out the door, hopping onto my bike and pedaling faster than I need to.

The school comes into view, and I park my bike towards the front, kicking it into a stop, and sliding down to my feet. My backpack swings behind me as I make my way into the school, sliding into the first class of the day.

History.

The first thing my eyes come in contact with is the large Mercator map plastered onto the center.

My pen rises to my lips as other students start to filter in, my eyes catching onto Ms. Wilson and Mr. Pham conversing at the front of the room.

The bell rings, startling me out of my thoughts, and Ms. Wilson claps her hands together from the front. I briefly glance around, and the room is eerily fuller than it was just moments ago.

"We're having a historically-based debate in this class," Ms. Wilson says with a grin, glancing over at Mr. Pham.

"Today's debate is going to revolve around a touchier subject so all we ask of you is to show respect to your peers." A wan smile. "According to our values here at Elkwood."

I almost have to laugh at that. The laugh bubbles up in my throat, but I'm able to keep it down, thankfully.

Somewhere across the room, the new girl, possible candidate, and shining beacon—Laura Johnson—catches my eyes, lips twitching slightly.

I bite my bottom lip. Laura here has been at Elkwood for a whole of three seconds, and even she can already tell that "*our values here at Elkwood*" do not consist of any respect whatsoever. If it did at some point, those values are long gone.

"So, Mr. Pham is going to write the topic on the board." Ms. Wilson says, nodding over to the shorter man who grabs a whiteboard marker, scribbling down a title.

Students squint, leaning from side to side in order to find a better angle. Once he steps aside, though, the title pops out of the whiteboard with smoldering intensity.

"Oh my God." One girl says.

Once my eyes find the writing, I can't help but find the girl's mutter of exclamation appropriate. Because, right there, smack in the middle of the whiteboard, it reads:

Should symbols of the Confederacy be taken down?

Brett laughs. Laura lets out a nearly imperceptible snort. For different reasons, I'm guessing.

"Lately, people have been taking down monuments due to the historical backgrounds of the figures depicted. Many institutions and companies are also banning the Confederate flag from their events. So, should we be taking these statues and symbols down? Or should we keep them up, regardless of individual opinions on said monuments?" Ms. Wilson asks, glancing about the audience as Mr. Pham gives a slight nod.

"Debate team," He says, "I'll be expecting you to step up, get this whole thing in motion. A difficult topic, but it'll be such an intriguing discussion to have."

Intriguing isn't necessarily the word I'd use.

"Okay, so," Brett starts, rising to his feet, letting hair fall off to the side and eliciting chuckles from the other students. "We should *not* be taking Confederate flags and symbols down."

I highly doubt that anyone was surprised at Brett's stance. At all.

He's so predictable these days, it nearly hurts.

"And why is that?" Ms. Wilson asks, slightly egging him on.

"Because it's *history.*" Brett throws his hands in the air like he's just made a ground-breaking point. "You can't just get rid of historical symbols because you don't like them."

Silence. Brett smirks. It's the usual, really. Brett makes a stupid point, and no one makes a move to challenge him. Ms. Wilson and Mr. Pham glance around the room. All mouths are shut. Nothing abnormal, really.

"*Actually,*" Someone's voice rings through the air. Everyone turns to the girl so quickly that I'm certain they get whiplash. The sound of someone else's voice is foreign to the group. After all, everyone is used to Brett monopolizing the entire conversation.

Laura Johnson is speaking.

"What's interesting is that you claim that people's hatred of the Confederate flag and other symbols are due to petty reasons such as *dislike.* I mean, that symbol is a symbol of white supremacy." She lets out a laugh, glancing around. "Isn't that common knowledge?"

The class glances to Brett, whose eyebrows are raised, lips slightly quirked downwards. It's like watching a tennis game, all our eyes bouncing back and forth between the two opposers.

"That's ridiculous," Brett laughs, haughtily. "Don't believe everything you read on leftist media. The Confederate flag was about the economy and Southern pride, not white supremacy."

"Incorrect," Laura cuts in, a wry grin appearing on her lips, raising her laptop upwards from where it is situated on her desk. "The creator of the Confederate flag— William T. Thompson— stated this in his own words, while describing the flag." Her eyes drop to her laptop screen, reading aloud. "'*As people, we are fighting to maintain the Heaven-ordained supremacy of the white man over the inferior or colored race.*'"

Audible gasps and whispers circulate the classroom.

There's a slight drain of color from Brett's face. "Where'd you get that off of? CNN?" He snorts, weaving around the desks, and peering over Laura's laptop.

"Nope. A historical document, actually. William T. Thompson. April 23, 1863." Laura says, lips pulled into a sardonic grin. "Would you like to hear the rest?"

Brett's eyes stay on the screen, eyes roving from left to right. "I mean," He shuffles away, back to his seat, eyes narrowed. "That doesn't mean you can stop people from exercising their right to freedom of speech and expression."

Laura raises both eyebrows, then sends me a glance, as if saying*: he can't be serious.*

"Uh, *hello?* Hate speech isn't protected under the right of free speech. You're kidding." Laura Johnson is a glass of fresh water. Her eyes alone speak cosmos. Those dark irises can make anyone watching her feel more alive.

"It's not hate speech," Brett's eyes narrow further, agitation creeping into his tone. "Don't be stupid."

Before Laura can open her mouth and effectively slam him down again— Ms. Wilson cuts in.

"Does anyone else want to pitch in?" A strained laugh. "As entertaining as this is, we can't have the two of you dominating the entire debate. Anyone?" She asks, glancing around.

Mr. Pham scans the room. I sink further into my chair. *Don't call on me, don't call on me—*

Mr. Pham glances in my direction. He smiles.

A string of curses fly through my mind. I attempt to blend in, but being the only black kid in the entire class forces me to stand out like a beacon.

"Amina!" He cries out, grin appearing as though he's just remembered that I'm also in the debate extracurricular.

My face goes hot, and I ponder how bad the fall will be if I make a split second decision to fling myself out of the nearest window. I'm tempted to see how it turns out.

"Amina." He repeats.

I blink.

"Any counter-arguments? Support?" He presses, and I let out a shaky breath, ignoring the eyes burning into me.

I glance over at Brett whose smug smirk is still plastered onto his lips.

"Brett," I start, surprising everyone in the room, myself included— "how many times have you seen the swastika showcased in Germany? On cars? Posters? License plates?"

The question causes eyes to widen and Mr. Pham to let out a low whistle.

"We're not *in* Germany." Brett replies, gaining a laugh of approval from one of the members of his group.

"And?" I ask, eyebrows scrunched together. "The swastika is a symbol of hate. It's *illegal* to display Nazi symbols in Germany," I state. "You can get thrown in *jail* for pulling that crap. It's a symbol of hate, just like the Confederate flag. Hate speech shouldn't be showcased."

"The Confederate flag isn't the same thing as the Swastika. They're from two different nations and carry two different histories and connotations." Brett says, arms folded.

Laura coughs, badly disguising a surprised exhale of amusement.

"What do you mean?" I ask, eyebrows scrunched. "Both of them are responsible for the mass murdering and abusing of innocent people. The swastika was the symbol of hate behind the Holocaust. The Confederate flag? A symbol of hate behind the mass enslavement, torture and abuse of black people."

Slight murmurs fill the air.

"It's not about slavery." Brett says, argument weakening by the second. "It was about wealth, money, the economy."

"How is it not?" I ask, a hand rising to the air. "Black people *were* the currency." I glance around the room. "The Confederacy wanted to keep enslaving black people. Sure, it benefited their economy, but these were *people*. And under the Confederacy's ideals, black people would remain slaves, remain sub-humans."

"That's not what the Confederacy wanted," Brett states, letting out a low laugh.

"Yes it did." I say. "That's why the whole Civil War started. The Confederacy wanted a state in which they could protect and preserve the institution of slavery." I pull out my laptop, pulling up the excerpt. "Alex Stephens—vice president of the Confederacy—literally stated that their new government was founded '*upon the great truth that the Negro is not equal to the white man; that slavery subordination to the superior race is his natural and normal condition.*'"

Someone swears, Brett blinks.

"And the Confederate flag? It was used by post-war racists to celebrate those who fought on the Confederate side. Generals, tacticians, you name it. Examples of them? Slave owners, abusers."

"Yeah? Give one example." Brett says, arms still folded.

"Easy." I say, "Robert E. Lee. Slave-owner. Documents reveal that he actually encouraged his overseers to cruelly beat and whip his slaves. To '*lay it on well*.' He wasn't a hero."

And he doesn't even scrape the *surface* of the malicious sea ravaged by Confederate generals and their rugged legacies.

Brett opens his mouth, closes it.

"They were also traitors to the country." This time it's Walt, and he stutters it out, meeting my eyes with one of those rigid shrugs of his. "I mean, they waged war against the United States, as we've learned in history class. By definition, that pretty much made them traitors to said country." He adjusts his glasses, blue veins sticking out from pale skin. "Dude, they *slaughtered* more than one-hundred-and-ten-thousand American soldiers."

Silence.

"And they lost," Laura dives back into the conversation. "They caused needless deaths, wanted to preserve slavery, and turned against said nation as a whole. Yet, I've never seen another state more proud of *losing* than the confederates."

"So, you're saying we should pretend all this never happened? May as well throw education down the drain." Brett shrugs, eyes cold, although he's losing ground.

And all the ground he's losing is ground that Laura Johnson is gaining. Ground that we're gaining.

"These statues were made to glorify these people." Walt replies, hands fidgeting with each other as though he doesn't know what to do with them. "There's a reason these symbols re-emerged under the Jim Crow era by white supremacists, lynching mobs, and the KKK."

Laura nods slowly, eyes flicking back to Brett. "No one is saying that we shouldn't learn about these people. But we can't glorify them.

Put them in textbooks, museums. Not army bases, and not parks." Laura finishes, arms crossed.

And they should *not* be preserved in the glorified statue forms that are meant to commemorate their vicious acts.

"And our great-grandparents? We're not allowed to be proud of their sacrifices, their fights?" Max Wright pitches in, eyebrows raised.

"Proud of what?" I ask, and his eyes flick over to mine. "The Confederate fighters? Slave-owners? People who fought for that?" *Abusers? Killers? White supremacists?* My hands seem to be shaking, and Max tilts his head over to the side, a scowl curling onto his lips.

"Yeah, no offense," Laura says, arms folding. "If that was the case, your great-grandparents might not exactly be your biggest flex." *Oohs* passes through the classroom, as Ms. Wilson blinks, turning to Laura. "Settle down, Miss Johnson."

"Like yours were perfect?" Max asks, leaning back in his seat.

"No one said that?" Laura knits her eyebrows together. "Although, I'm proud of my roots, proud of my heritage, proud that they *weren't* Confederate terrorists."

Max Wright rises to his feet, hands slamming the table, facing burning red. He's lost his cool in seconds. Meanwhile, Laura Johnson is as calm as usual, eyeing him with ocean-like neutrality.

"Off topic," Mr. Pham says, a strained grin appearing on his lips. "No need to bring anybody's grandparents into this." A light laugh.

"A very intense debate," Ms. Wilson chuckles, as if we aren't *actually* having an argument about why slave-owners and abusers should *not* be celebrated. "There were very strong points made from both sides."

I blink repeatedly at Ms. Wilson's last sentence.

Laura's eyebrows practically shoot upwards, and I'm sure mine do too. Meanwhile, Brett still glares daggers at her, standing next to Max Wright, both looking equally irritated.

And an hour later, the bell rings.

No one makes a move at first, but Mr. Pham diplomatically wraps up the painful debate, insisting that it's a difficult topic, and about how there are no straight answers to something this controversial.

They act like it's difficult to see it for what it is. I'm certain Mr. Pham is well aware, but he has to be *nice Mr. Pham, friendly Mr. Pham.*

He finishes by encouraging other kids to contribute to the conversation. Once he's done, the students start mindlessly packing their bags, making their way out of the classroom. They send Laura brief glances as she carefully shoves her things into her backpack, not taking notice of the intense eyes on her.

I follow suit, receiving a tight lipped grin from both of the teachers. Laura makes her way to the door as well. She glances up at me, as though she's about to say something.

That is, until she's shoved into my side.

Max Wright lets out a laugh as he and the White Bros™ shuffle through the door as one collective pack.

"Whoops." Brett says from the front, eyeing Laura with a brief shrug, smirk snake-like on his lips."Might want to watch where you're going, Johnson."

My lips part.

Laura laughs.

"Sorry about that," I say to her, eyebrows knitting as I watch the pack of wolves shuffle through the hallway.

"Don't be." A smirk curves onto her lips as she casts me a determined glance.

"Why is that?" I ask, shoulders bumping as we make our way through the hallway.

Laura's determined glance almost intensifies, a steady resolve rising to her widening smirk. "Because you're going to help me beat him."

the melting pot

I scream.

Pulling my burning palm away from the steel pot, I flick my wrist back and forth. A laugh reverberates through the kitchen as Ms. King smooths down a lengthy skirt.

"Don't tell me you burnt water again," She says slowly, eyes crinkling at the sides as she smiles.

"One time," I say, as Ms. King— or *Gran* as she prefers me to refer to her as— hands me a cold compress.

"Just press it against your arm, will you?" She asks, Barbadian accent peeking through her melodic voice. I take the ice, pressing it against the developing bruise and exhaling a hiss.

She analyzes me for a few moments, eyes flicking between me and the ice, shaking her head as amusement drips from her dark features. She mutters something in Bajan, and I purse my lips.

"So," I start, my eyes travelling to the boiling pot. "Should I put that on the stove or—?"

"Yeah, no." She laughs, bustling about the restaurant kitchen. "See, I'm trying not to get you killed today."

"Oh, today?"

"I only try to kill you on Tuesdays, you know that." She places her hands on my shoulder. "Time for you to leave, dearheart."

"Fine," I let my shoulders sag as Gran pushes me out of the kitchen. "Wait." I say, and we both come to a halt. Ducking underneath her shoulder, I head over to a counter, grabbing a rounded pastry from one of the plates. Waving it in the air, I wink. "Thanks, Gran."

She places her hands on her hips, shaking her head as I speed out of the kitchen, dark curls rising to the air.

"If I catch you—" Gran says, waving a finger into the air, while simultaneously not going after me. She's interesting like that. Acts tough, yet goes easy. After all, Gran's known me since I was born. To her, I'm another grandchild.

The door to the restaurant kitchen shuts behind me and a grin rises to my lips as I head out into the open space, scanning the area for my parents.

The diner is checkered in red and white squares, small and cosy, dim lighting, and busy as usual. The usual customers are seated in the patterned seats, their usual orders sat atop their plates.

Once a month, my family visits the diner, taking a seat at our usual round table in the center. Ms. Alvarez is seated on a high chair, digging into her lunch of chicken alfredo penne pasta while ranting about the corruption in her own country to her best friend, one Ms. Cruz, both of them barking out laughter every so often. Towards the right, you'll see Mr. Asfour seated next to his wife, both of them speaking quickly and rapidly, leaning back in their chairs as their son chirps into the conversation every few seconds.

Miss Silva's always here as well, close cut black curls paired with hoop earrings, talking to Mr. Willis, a soft-spoken dark-skinned man, both of them sharing their vast travelling experiences.

Ms. Bulan is seated in her wheelchair towards the front table, white hair wispy and contrasting to her olive tawny skin, speaking to teenaged Orion as he wipes a glass cup, nodding ever so often, dark curls glinting beneath the lighting.

The diner, in all respects, is a melting pot.

We work like a well oiled machine, going to the front to grab our usual orders whenever Orion rings the bell, signalling that they're ready. Orion has always been a constant presence, rich brown skin nodding to the Ojibwe and Black in him.

There's a multitude of different cuisines in the diner, more nations represented than I've ever seen in the school cafeteria menu.

It seems like we all congregate in this one space, conversing in a flurry of different languages.

Mrs. Stoica walks in, smoothing down her usual floral dress, shouting out a greeting to everyone who's already seated inside before making her way to her usual seat, to talk to Ms. Zhao who waves her over.

Claudie runs around with Ms. Alvarez' son, Santi, and Mrs. Levitt's son, Amos, the three of them speeding under tables and around chairs to catch each other.

The bustle of the diner brings an upwards curve to my lips, the relief of finally being done with ALO settling in. I scan the area. Travel and politics rise to the electric atmosphere and dominate it.

When my eyes latch onto where my parents are seated, all dark curls and bright eyes, I slide into the seat across from them.

I dive into conversation with them instantly. The conversation travels to the new girl—Laura Johnson—and her plans to run for president, alongside the history debate that elicited even more maliciousness from Brett and his friends.

"So, I'm helping her run for president," I say to my parents, flatbread in hand as I take a bite out of it. I'm filling my parents in on the plan to help Laura run for president, and they listen attentively, nodding every so often.

"Not a bad idea," Dad says, tilting his head to the side.

"I recommend asking Ms. Cruz about it," Mom says, daintily pressing on her lips with a napkin, "She has a degree in political science, you know?"

"Yeah. In fact, I'm sure everyone here would have some good advice on the topic." Dad says while scanning the diner, drink in hand.

Surveying the diner, I nod to my parents' advice, making a mental note about who to ask and when to ask them. Before I can speak up again, the front door opens hesitantly, causing everyone's eyes to turn to the people in front.

My cup almost falls from my hand when I see that it's Emory. Emory Richards. Despite him being one of the few visible minorities in the town, it never crossed my mind that I'd see him here.

Ever.

His presence makes it seem like both of my worlds are colliding, and I'm not too sure how I feel about it.

An older woman is next to him, brown curls falling to her shoulder, tawny skin similar to her son's, brown eyes scanning the diner with slight apprehension.

His mom makes her way to the front counter, Emory trailing behind her as she orders something from Orion who scribbles something down in his notebook.

Emory glances around the diner.

"He's wearing the Elkwood uniform," Mom muses, caressing her chin.

"That must be Emory, then," Dad says, leaning backwards in his seat as he analyzes him.

Emory's mom nods briefly after placing her order before she retraces her steps, scanning around the diner as if looking for a place to sit. Mom and Dad exchange glances before Mom raises a polite hand, waving her over to our joint table.

Our table seats about six, and so, there's enough room for Emory's mom to sit across my parents, and for Emory to sit across from me.

Our parents plunge into polite conversation, and I purse my lips at them before turning back to Emory and giving him an awkward nod.

He nods back at me, fingers adjusting his school vest, the Elkwood emblem at the top right.

He opens his mouth before closing it again, eyes squinting in thought. After a few seconds, he speaks up.

"Did you know that Brett's running for president?" He asks, eyes steady.

"Yeah," I exhale, "He more-or-less dropped the news to Laura and I during lunch."

There's a few moments of silence. Amber's going to be vexed

when she finds out. The elections are definitely going to be tense with Amber and Brett at each other's throats, vying for the head seat at the StuCo table. Although, Brett's announcement doesn't seem like a sudden change of plans.

Elections have always been tense, after all. Strange how the intelligent and attractive are thrust onto the electoral playing field like gladiators. Elkwood elections are always in pairs: student council president is bestowed upon the person with the highest votes, and the role of vice president is slid over to the runner up.

However, people like Amber and Brett do not vy for second best. When the world has always taught you that you're number one, second place isn't even in the equation. Laura Johnson, however, is also not settling for second. Not because the world told her she is worth more than second place, but because she told the world that she is worth more than second.

"It was sudden, I guess." Emory says, distractedly, drumming the table with his fingers.

I knit my eyebrows together. "It seems that way."

However, I doubt it was. I doubt that Brett hearing Laura's plan to run for president was what made him make that split second decision. In fact, I doubt that it was a split second decision at all.

I dip my flatbread into the white bowl of hummus, humming in thought. Amber was putting a lot of effort into staying in Brett's good books so that she'd eradicate her only major possible competition from the elections.

However, I don't think that Brett was going to back down so easily. I don't think he was going to just give Amber a free run while he watched from the sidelines.

It's not *like* him. Not when he's constantly acting like he's God's very own gift to the world, not when his smirks are always dripping with *better-than-you* condescension and his head is held up ridiculously high like everyone around him is a mere speck in the universe, while he's the center of it all.

Brett was always going to run, I realize. He was playing Amber, which isn't all that surprising. I mean, this is Brett MsSomething we're talking about. Messing around with people is his hobby.

Still, Amber was completely fooled into thinking that she'd have an easy run.

Or maybe she didn't actually believe Brett was going to stand aside. I shake my head. In fact, maybe it was just hope driving her up until now. *Hope* that Brett would let her have this. *Hope* that she'd coast through the election process and garner all the votes.

Either way, the stakes have been upped in the competition. I have no idea how I'm going to bring the new girl, Laura, to the coveted seat at the StuCo table, but I already know that I'm intent on doing so, regardless of the competition that Brett and Amber pose.

"So," Emory drags the word out, "You're helping the new girl run?" There's a doubtful tone to his voice that I choose to brush away.

"Yeah," I say with a nod as Emory's food is placed in front of him and he pulls out his cutlery.

"Well," He says, taking a swig out of a bottle of Sprite, "This year's elections are going to be interesting."

His eyes shine with something like amusement, slightly coated in thought. He's also completely right about that. Never once have the stakes been so high. Never once has an outsider fought for the bid for presidency. Never once have two insanely powerful teenagers run against each other, possibly severing their allyship in the process.

It's more than just a new year. It's a new Elkwood. I can tell that it's not just me who thinks so, because Emory's lips twitch slightly as his words sprinkle the air.

I nod, eyes steady and shoulders slightly rolled back.

"Agreed."

campaign week

"So, where we headed, Manager?" Laura asks, eyes scouting the hall as the remainder of the students start heading out for today. I push the door to the art room open, leaning off to the side to let Laura pass through.

"The art room," I reply with a half grin, watching as Laura makes her way into the space.

The art teacher—Mr. Ingram—allowed us access to the art room for about an hour. I make my way over to the center table. Right now, the main thing we need is to make up for lost time and start making posters.

Splashes of paint decorate the room and Laura roams the shelves for additional supplies to the ones I have. When we make our way back to the table, we lay out posters, lips pursed as we imagine how the campaign posters should look.

"God, we won't have time to finish all these." Laura says after a few minutes, placing a paintbrush back into a water-filled vase.

I let out a breath, eyes scanning over the posters. "We might."

Laura bites her lip, shaking her head. "I just narrowly handed in my form before the deadline yesterday. We're walking on a thin rope here."

"We'll get it done," I say with a nod, eyes steady on hers. When she doesn't say anything more, I say, "We can pull an all-nighter." Or more. "Trust me when I say we'll get it all done."

A firm, uncharacteristic confidence laces my tone, and Laura returns with a nod. Then we're back to the posters, painting streaks across the papers, discussing slogans, and scrutinizing artistic decisions.

Music fills the air, blasting from Laura's phone, and minutes blur into over an hour. Realizing that we've spent one and a half hours in the art room—an hour longer than Mr. Ingram permitted—I scramble to my feet, shuffling the dried posters into one pile and shoving them under my arm.

Realization dawns on Laura's features and she rises to her feet as well, hanging the wet posters from the clothes pegs on the art room's ceiling.

"So, the posters are essentially handled," Laura says as we walk out of the art classroom, shutting off the lights and making our way down the hall.

"We can finish them up within..." I hum, "The next two days, tops."

"Then... " Laura says as we hoist our backpacks onto our shoulders and push our way out of the school doors and into the chilly air, "We can focus on the next aspect of my campaign."

We exchange half grins. Because the next goal is arguably the most important, and could change the course of Laura's campaign as we know it:

Winning over the student body.

***

"Is it true that you're running?" It's probably the twelfth or so time this question has been asked today. My eyes drift upwards to see one Yasmine Abadi standing by my table, arms folded as her eyes stay on Laura's.

Somehow, slight guilt needles at my chest. With everything that's happened: the awkward lunch with Yasmine's friends, breaking off with ALO, and helping Laura run for president, I haven't gotten the chance to talk to Yasmine again.

Or maybe, a voice says, *you didn't put in the effort.*

Laura nods as she rests her chin on her hand, giving Yasmine a simple, "Yeah, I am."

Yasmine's eyes touch mine for a second, and I speak up. "Y-you can sit with us."

She purses her lips at that, her eyebrows raising slightly. "Oh, has Amber allowed that?"

My shoulders sag, and I give her a look. "*Yasmine.*"

"*Amina*." She echoes, and Laura's eyes dart between the two of us, eyebrows quirked.

"I broke it off with Amber," I say. "It wasn't the best collaboration." *Understatement.* "A lot went down," I twirl my fork in my bowl of ramen. An exhale as a crooked grin rises to my lips. "I want you to sit with us. Please. If you want to."

Yasmine's lips twitch. "Cool with you?" She asks, turning to Laura.

"Sure," Laura says through bites of her pierogis, giving her a thumbs up.

With that, Yasmine lowers herself into the seat next to me, arms folded over the table.

"We're trying to work out who to gear Laura's campaign towards." I say, glancing over at Yasmine.

"Who's easier to sway," Laura nods, jutting a fork in the air.

"Oh, that's right," Yasmine says, a hand rising to her forehead. "It's Campaign Lunch."

I nod. Campaign Lunch has always been a tradition at Elkwood, for as long as I can remember. It's the lunch where all the candidates try to outdo each other with splendor and attention-grabbers, all to win over the student body.

Whoever catches the most attention during Campaign Lunch has the highest likelihood of winning the coveted spot of president.

You have to be outstanding, and you have to push boundaries. Every word, every glance counts. You need to bridge the chasm between the student government and the student body.

Yasmine scans the cafeteria with a hum. "My table might be swayed to vote for you," She hums again, "And the theatre kids are always out to break the social hierarchy, so you can count on them voting; mainly out of spite for Amber and her group, though."

Laura's eyes scan over the two aforementioned tables, and she takes all the information in, nodding slowly, before saying. "Although, those two tables voting for me will be great, it won't be enough to win Brett and his group."

"Some people might be getting tired of always seeing Amber and Brett at the top," I nod towards the Ambiguous Whites, who eat across from each other. Golden and silver bracelets curve around the girls' wrists, and a thin chain or two hangs from the guys' necks, some brandishing the crucifix.

"They can be double sided when it comes to Amber and Brett." I say, eyes steady on them, before turning back to Yasmine and Laura. "If we can win them over, or somehow, butter them into supporting us, they might just vote to spite Amber."

"So... there's a lot more at play here," Laura hums, tilting her head to the side. "I'm betting we can win some of them over."

Her eyes are calculating, self-assured. It almost seems like she's in a trance, before her hand clamps down on the table, Yasmine's spine straightening at the sound.

"Let's hand out my flyers." Laura says, packing her black sheen of hair into a braid, and rising from the table.

So, we do.

We hand out the flyers, drifting from table to table. Yasmine hands out flyers to her table first, I make sure to dish them out to the drama kids, (albeit awkwardly), and Laura makes her way to the most uncomfortable tables, being the Ambiguous Whites and of course, Brett and Amber's table. Despite the skeptical look on those students' faces, Laura hands them her flyers with a confidence that makes it seem like she's gone to this school her whole life.

It's clear that there's discomfort within Amber and Brett's table. With Brett's last minute bid for the same spot Amber's vying for, the White Bros™ and ALO seem to have an uncomfortable divide, apparent by ALO sitting further towards the edge of the table while the White Bros™ congregate around Brett, making jokes that they laugh heartily to.

"What's this?" Tyler asks, holding Laura's flyer in hand, eyes roaming over it.

"My flyers," Laura says, easily, "For my campaign."

A redhead near him laughs, letting out a swear. "You're kidding," His eyes widen, "I thought it was a rumour."

"Yeah," One quips, "Or that Brett was just messing around with us."

Tyler slides the flyer back onto the table. "Sorry, What's-Your-Face, but I've gotta vote for Brett. Nothing personal, though."

Brett chuckles. "You're *actually* handing out flyers at this table?"

I make my way over to Laura, hands clasped. "Well, *this table*'s part of the student body, so it's worth a shot."

"Right," Brett drawls, "Well, you'd have better luck convincing the girls." He says, glancing at where ALO is seated at the far end of the table, scouting the scene with passive expressions.

"Then again, it's not like they're up for conversation," He chuckles. "Amber's still butthurt that I'm running for president."

Leslie mutters something to Amber who decidedly ignores Brett's comment, rising to her feet with a container filled with perfectly cut brownies.

At this point, Yasmine shuffles over to where Laura and I are standing by Brett's table.

"She's seriously buying people over," Yasmine says, eyes on Amber as the girl shuffles from table to table, handing out brownies to people seated at the surrounding tables, pointedly avoiding Brett and his friends despite their loud protests.

She returns to the table, leaning against it, eyes traveling over the White Bros™, Leslie and Olivia on either side of her. "If you guys want any of these, think carefully about who you're voting for."

Groans fill the table as Leslie gives the boys unimpressed looks. The cafeteria hushes only slightly, eyes drawn to the scene. Brett lets out a bark of laughter, rising to his feet and standing on top of his chair. He scans the entire cafeteria before pointing at Amber.

Campaign Lunch has officially commenced.

"Is this who you want for your president?" He asks, smirk smug as he eyes the audience. Olivia gives Amber a nervous nudge, and I exchange glances with both Yasmine and Laura. Brett plows on, "Do you want someone as petty as Amber Wesley?" Amber blanches from where she stands, but Brett remains unfazed, "Someone who tries to manipulate people into voting for her. Someone who tries to buy you off with *brownies*?"

Murmurs fill the cafeteria.

"Has Elkwood lost every last shred of respectability to the point where you can be bought with *brownies*? To the point where someone as over-emotional and over-dramatic as Amber can win for president?" He shakes his head. "Look at her. I don't know if it's that time of the month or something, but she's out of control." He says, still smirking, eliciting laughter from the White Bros™.

My lips part, and ALO, Yasmine, and Laura mirror my expression.

Brett continues, "I'm serious, though. It has to be. I mean, Amber's so *triggered* right now, and it's not like it's anything unusual, guys. She's lost it. If she's president and someone so much as *questions* her, she's going to be impulsive and bring Elkwood's StuCo down with her." He laughs.

"She doesn't know anything about politics whatsoever." Brett goes on, then he turns to a stoplight-red Amber. "Next time, sweetheart, stick to bikini Instagram pics. Presidency isn't for someone like you."

Utter silence.

Amber's tray of brownies falls to the floor, and her hands tremble as she heads out of the cafeteria, breaths coming out in quick gusts, Leslie and Olivia following her out of the cafeteria doors.

"Wow," Laura says, eyes softening once the doors shut behind them.

He *dragged* her.

Brett lets out a laugh, stepping down from the seat in favour of sitting on it, instead. The White Bros™ praise him with high fives and loud barks of laughter.

Murmurs fill the cafeteria, and my eyes latch onto Walt, who's randomly handing out pins for his campaign, going ignored by the majority of the student body.

"Is this what you do here?" Laura asks, drawing the cafeteria's attention to her.

"Yeah," Tyler laughs, receiving pats on the back for his intelligent comeback.

Laura shakes her head, making eye contact with every student who drops their gaze from her. "You shame someone out of running?" She lets out a dry laugh. " I thought this was all a fair game."

Brett scoffs, but she ignores him.

"And maybe it's just me, but how many girls here were cool with Brett's '*that time of the month*' comment?"

No one raises a hand. Girls exchange glances.

"It was disrespectful, that's what it was." She turns to Brett who's leaning back in his chair. "You know it's *possible* for you to debate with someone without tearing them down, or using sexist comments to shut them up."

Brett nudges his friends, and Laura turns away from him.

"I'm serious. Brett didn't make any good points, all he did was draw attention to Amber, instead of telling us how and why he's going to be a good president."

Ad hominem. A classic strategy; tearing down the opponent, rather than their argument.

Laura glances towards me and I clear my throat, attempting not to squirm under the hundreds of eyes on me.

"A vote for Laura is a vote for everyone's voices being heard," I say, scanning each and every face. "It's a vote for an open discussion instead of shutting someone down." Pause. I gesture towards Brett. "I mean, aren't you tired of Brett controlling Elkwood?" Murmurs fill the cafeteria. "Aren't you tired of him comfortably sitting at the top with no competition? Where there's no one to challenge him or hold him accountable?"

Some hums come from the Ambiguous Whites' table.

"Aren't you tired of seeing the same old face? Only having one option?" Yasmine pitches in, hands resting on her hips.

"That's the problem with so many places right now. There's only *one* option." Laura emphasizes, eyes catching mine.

"There's no balance, no opposition. It's actually what we fear the most about dictatorships." I say.

That's when Brett stops exaggeratedly mouthing along to what we're saying and rises to his feet. "Oh okay, so you're comparing me to a dictator, now?"

"No one is doing that." Laura says, brushing Brett's outburst to the side. "What we're doing is giving you something new, something different. Something refreshing. I want that. This country wants that. A new candidate is past overdue at this school."

Laura's grabbing their attention. Her hands wave around as her entire stance commands the entire cafeteria's focus.

"A vote for Laura is a vote for something new, something different. A vote for Laura means a much needed change happening at this school. A vote for Laura means all of you," Passion infuses her lungs and dark eyes, and she outstretches her hands to the audience, "And I mean *all* of you," She nods towards the forgotten kids lingering around the cafeteria. "Will have your voices heard."

Laura breathes heavily when done, and it almost seems like a mic drop moment.

Then there's silence; uneasy, unsure silence. Deafening silence. The students stare up at her, eyes widened as if this is the first time they've heard a speech. Someone talking directly *to* them instead of *at* them.

In seconds, something sharp punctures through the thundering silence after what feels like an eternity.

Emory Richards is clapping. As in, hands-together, chin-up, head-nodding, clapping.

I almost let out a frenzied laugh as the isolated clapping travels from table to table, and Laura beams, an arm finding my shoulder. My lips part as I make eye-contact with Yasmine, because soon, what was once scarce clapping becomes thunderous applause, louder than any silence I've ever witnessed.

when nat visits

I take a sip out of my icy lemonade, using a spoon to stir the drink for no real reason whatsoever. I'm out in the front porch, seated on a washed-out chair, eyes scanning the backyard, cup in hand.

After the rollercoaster that was today, it takes a lot for me to relax for a few moments, processing everything that went down at

Campaign Lunch. In all honesty, it looks like the student body might actually want Laura for president.

The speech itself sent chills down my spine, and I wouldn't be surprised if all the avid listeners had the same experience. Campaign Lunch went impossibly well for us.

I take another drink of my juice, letting blocks of ice cool my mouth, and the soft wind caress my face. For once, it feels like I'm actually winning.

"Why are you so happy?" Claudie chirps, skipping out onto the backyard deck and sliding onto the seat next to me.

"Some good things happened today," I say with a shrug as Claudie adjusts her butterfly adorned t-shirt, raising a plastic cup to her lips.

"Why are *you* so happy?" I ask as Claudie hums to some nursery song.

"No reason." She says, beaded braids swinging back and forth with her every movement.

I give her a look, and she breaks out into a grin.

"Miss Stacy says that I could be in the spelling bee in a couple of weeks."

"That's so cool, Claudie." I say, a smile curving onto my lips.

"Yeah, I know," She says, matter of factly, slipping off of the chair and heading back into the house.

I let out a laugh. *Apparently* this conversation is over.

I down the rest of the drink, checking my phone to see the latest updates on the campaign. Posters, Laura's slogans, and the flyers are the main things that appear on the screen.

In someone's Instagram story, a clip of Laura's speech is playing, and a smile curves onto my lips. I set my drink to the side, freezing when I hear an ear-splitting scream.

Claudie's.

As though on fire, I jump to my feet, running into the house and to the living room when I see him.

He's surrounded by the rest of my family, all hovering around him and shooting him questions. Once my eyes land on him, I release a matching scream and speed walk to where he is.

Because there he is; Nathaniel Davis, and he's standing right in our foyer.

***

"So, it's really different from here," Nat concludes, shoving spoonfuls of jambalaya into his mouth.

His college is all the way on the other side of the country, and everything about it opposes Elkwood and the entire state, to be honest.

For one, where you see MAGA merch here, you'll see *The Future is Female* and *Melanin* t-shirts over there. The city Nat currently resides and our town appear to be polar opposites, and Nat seems happier there, happier than I've ever seen him.

Nat's taller than the last time I've seen him, too. He's now standing at a solid 6' 3" in height. Might not be something to compare to NBA players, but he towers over my 5' 8".

"I trust you're staying safe," Dad says to Nat, his eyes gentle but firm.

Nat chuckles, letting out a breath. "I'm telling you, Dad, things are different there. It's not *like* here."

"Well, better to be safe than sorry," Mom says, lips pulled into a half grin as she shrugs.

Nat just shakes his head with a laugh. "Of course. Trust me."

"Can you take me with you when you leave?" Claudie asks, arms slung around Nat despite our parents' requests for her to sit down.

"Of course," Nat says, messing up her braids, "I'll just pack you up in my suitcase."

A bright grin rises to Claudie's face. "That should work."

Conversation continues to travel throughout the table, laughs filling the air. Nat makes a request for us to get rid of the rest of his old things, waving a dismissive hand and saying, "I don't need them anymore."

Mom nods at the request, eyes inquisitive before the conversation morphs from subject to subject.

"Could you walk with me to school tomorrow?" I ask after a few minutes of talking.

Nat nods as Mom gives me an unimpressed look, saying through a glance that I should let Nat rest after his long flight.

I'm surprised that Nat hasn't immediately refused, especially since I know how he gets about his sleep, and he's never handled long flights well either.

"Of course," Nat says with a grin, white teeth contrasting against his dark brown skin, "Just like we used to."

***

Walking to school with Nat brings back the feeling of sugary saccharine nostalgia. Suddenly, I'm 12 and Nat's 16, and I'm complaining about all the extra drama of sixth grade, while Nat listens.

Four years later, nothing's changed.

He's always been a good listener.

Nat walks down the sidewalk with an easy stride, raising his eyebrows when a middle-aged lady walking her dog casts him a weary look.

He lets out a breath, exchanging glances with me as the lady sidles to the edge of the sidewalk, tugging her poor dog along with her, eyes suspicious and cutting.

Nat laughs when she's gone, but there's no mirth to it. "Good to be back."

I nudge him with my shoulder. "A bit different than your new home."

Nat draws his lips into a line. "Almost forgot how it was."

"There's no place to escape it," I say with a shrug, clinging onto the straps of my backpack and letting my shoulders sag.

"True," Nat ruffles a hand through lustrous curls, all combed into his signature *Fresh-Prince-of-Bel Air-esque* fade. "It's just not as bad as it is here." He adjusts his plain t-shirt. "It's just sad, you know? For you to have to call this place home."

I'm about to say something reassuring when his choice of words plays over in my head.

"I'll miss y'all when I go back." He says, Air Force 1s tapping against the pavement. He ruffles my hair, letting my braids become tousled, but when I see his face, his smile is almost forlorn.

I shoulder his arms off of my shoulders, eyes cutting into him. My voice sounds dejected, weak, barely audible when I say, "You're not coming back."

Not a question, not a proposition. A statement.

My brother's eyes widen slightly, mouth opening and closing in hesitation before a fake, "don't be stupid," Comes out of his mouth, and a faux grin attempts to peek out. He reaches out for me, but I jump back as if burned.

"Don't lie to me, Nat." I say, venom tracing my voice.

Because, it isn't fair.

It's not fair that my brother's leaving, it's not fair that he isn't telling me, it's not fair that he isn't coming back. It's not fair that he'll never come back, and I'll be stuck here for years.

It's not fair that he has a new life in a new state, and I can see it in his eyes that he may not be planning on seeing me in person again.

Even if I *were* to follow him to the other side of the country, what then? He'd have graduated, and I'd be wandering the university halls, trying to catch the scent of my older brother from when he used to go there. I will never be able to walk to school with him again, filling him in on everything. Not only that, but my highlight of the year—Nat's annual visit—will be no more, and that hurts more than I care to admit.

Above all, it's not fair that I'm angry at him because I want to leave just as much as he does.

Yet he's not taking me with him.

***

I arrive at school alone, having ditched Nat in the middle of the sidewalk after my outburst. Laura catches my eye and speedwalks over to me, forcing me to push all my desolate thoughts away, focusing on the task at hand.

She's smiling, so I force myself to mirror her expression, and not think about the fact that my brother's never coming home again.

"We're doing so well," She says eagerly, hands raised in excitement. "I might actually win this thing."

We walk through the hallway, noticing Yasmine at her locker. Once she locks it shut, she grins at us, shuffling over to us.

"Texted the kids at my table, and the vast majority of them say that they're voting for you," Yasmine says.

Millie walks by, sending a beam towards Laura as she mindlessly tugs her kilt down and adjusts her messy red bun. She glances at me, shrugs and waves, a gesture that I return, albeit hesitantly.

My eyes return to Laura and before I can ask, she speaks up.

"I've been talking to all the kids in our grade." She says, nodding at someone as they pass by, "Having one-on-one conversations with them, in the hallways and while walking."

"That's really good," I say with a nod and a grin that looks happier than I feel.

"They feel like they know me personally." Laura emphasizes.

"That's the key," Yasmine says as she nods, "You win over the individual, you win over the collective."

"And apparently," Laura says conspiratorially, dropping her voice. "The bad blood between Amber, Brett, and the kids two tables away from us," *The Ambiguous Whites,* I think as Laura finishes, "runs a lot deeper than we thought."

Yasmine raises a perfect eyebrow. "Pray tell."

Laura fills us in on the Ambiguous Whites, and the fact that the majority of them promised her their votes because of the one-sided rivalry.

Before I can take another step forward, a tall brunette stands in front of me. I look up to see Leslie Brown, skin pale as usual, hair packed back into an intense ponytail, blue eyes almost emotionless.

I make a move to curve around her, but she stops me, grabbing onto my wrist.

"Uh, Leslie?" I ask, attempting to tug my arm out of her grip.

"Wait," She says, and I exchange glances with Laura and Yasmine, both of whom are equally confused.

"Amber dropped out," Leslie says, letting my arm drop from her grip and folding both of her arms, eyes steady on us.

"I'm sorry, she did what?" Laura asks, squinting.

"I said what I said," Leslie says, letting out a breath. "Brett kind of got to her. He also played dirty with blackmail." She rolls her eyes. "He said—*and I quote*—that if we make things difficult, he's going to tell the principal that we were 'cyberbullying' Millie."

She sounds incredulous at that, and I raise my eyebrows. They *were* cyberbullying Millie, so Leslie's air quotes don't make much sense to me.

"Do you know what's in the school code for cyberbullying?" She asks, eyes intense. "A week-long suspension, possibly *expulsion.*" She lets out a dry laugh. "Our campaign is ruined. And honestly," Leslie shakes her head, staring at the ground. "This time Brett went too far."

"Understatement," Yasmine says through feigned coughs, causing Leslie to scoff in something resembling agreement.

"So..." I trail off, as if asking, *what are we supposed to do with this information?*

"I'm sure you're all ecstatic." Leslie says, icy eyes walking up and down our trio.

Laura shakes her head, saying resignedly, "Come on, Leslie. No one wants to win like that."

"Whatever," Leslie says, hands tracing the school emblem on the top right of her navy blue school vest. "I'm just asking all of you to do *one* thing."

I cast a glance at Laura, pursing my lips.

"And that would be?" Yasmine asks, drumming her fingertips on her dark pants.

Leslie curls her lips into something uncomfortably resembling a sneer: "Beat him."

My mouth opens to form some sort of reply as my eyes drift from Leslie. When my gaze latches onto something in the distance, all my words fall dead in my throat and my mouth parts in shock.

Emory is walking into the school, students gaping as he walks by, because a purple bruise covers his right eye, and nasty red splotches decorate his face.

And with that, Leslie's requirement falls to deaf ears, and my heart threatens to pound out of my chest because Emory Richards has been attacked.

had it coming

The cafeteria is abuzz for the following reasons:

1. The upcoming elections and Laura's surprisingly good chances of securing StuCo presidency. Every once in a while, someone drops by our table to affirm that they're rooting for Laura.

2. Emory Richards having gotten beaten up, and speculations about what may've happened to him. One of the most popular assumptions being that Emory got into a fight with a gang.

(As if there are any gangs in this state—outside of the mafia of course, and the frat boys.)

3. Emory Richards' absence from the White Bros™ table. At Elkwood, you don't switch tables. At all. Especially not when you're a regular at Brett's table. I'm serious. They're like a cult; when you go in, you can't get out.

4. The audible tension between ALO and the White Bros™ at their table, which consists of a multitude of snide comments exchanged between the two groups.

"I can't believe this," Yasmine says, hands clasped on top of the table, the light catching on the silver rings slid onto her fingers.

"Is it usually this chaotic?" Laura asks, not removing her gaze from her phone as her fingers fly across the screen.

Stress doodles make up my sheet of paper, and I hum, holding a pen to my lips before responding. "This is crazy, even by Elkwood standards." I finally get out.

Yasmine's eyes drift away from me to something behind me. "It gets crazier."

"How?" I ask, whipping around to look in the direction of her gaze. It's Emory, hands in pocket, gaze on the floor, lips pulled into a line. He walks directly past Brett's table, ignoring the jeers from the White Bros™ as he does so.

Gazes subtly travel to his lean figure, eyes calculating where he's going next. Emory runs a hand through his curls before whipping around as if he's heading out of the cafeteria.

"Wait!" Laura calls out, waving a hand in the air, the other hand pressing her phone to the table. Emory turns around, raising a finger to his chest. Laura nods quickly, ignoring the curious gazes of the students.

Emory stays still for a moment, debating something with himself before he lets his shoulders sag in resignation and he takes strides over to our table.

Yasmine moves her bag from the seat next to her, lowering it to the floor and allowing Emory to take the seat next to her.

"Hey," He says, letting out an exhausted breath. Our eyes just stay on him, analyzing the marks and bruises spotting his face.

“Are you okay?” I ask, stupidly. Emory gives me a look, eyebrows raised as if trying to decipher if I’m serious or not. I amend, “What happened? If you feel comfortable sharing.”

Emory leans back in his seat, dry grin curving onto his lips. “What do you think happened?” His eyes carefully drift over to Brett’s table and he shrugs.

“They didn’t.” Laura says, her words slow and enunciated.

“They did.” He chuckles with a nod.

“Please tell me the other guy looks worse. Or you put up a fight. At least.” Yasmine says, sliding a ring off of her pinky finger.

Emory laughs. “I was outnumbered. They were feeling salty,” He shrugs, “Not a big deal.”

Except, it is.

When he doesn’t receive a response from any of us, he speaks again. “They invited me over for a barbecue in Elkwood Park. They were vaping. Not a smoker, so I didn’t. And you know, they started roughhousing, got out of control with the lighters, and then...” He gracefully gestures to the bruises—which we now know are burn marks—on his face.

"That's disgusting," Laura says, at the same time I say, "It wasn't an accident," and something in my stomach curls in disgust.

"Oh, it definitely wasn't." Emory says, casually. "They all started messing with me, you know, pushing and tackling me in particular; that wasn't a coincidence." He purses his lips, tilting his head to the side. "Brett was behind it, anyways. Because he's butthurt about people actually standing up against him and—God forbid—having a different opinion than him."

"They can't just do things like that," Yasmine says, meeting Emory's eyes. He shrugs.

Except they can, and they'll get away with it.

"Yeah, well, it's fine." He says. "I didn't lay a finger on them, so I won't get reported or anything."

"*They* should get reported," Laura says, face tinged with a subtle pink.

"Listen, it doesn't matter," Emory laughs, lowly, "Give it a couple of weeks, and I'll be back to looking like a handsome devil."

He's the only one that's laughing—albeit lowly—and Laura doesn't seem satiated with his assurance. She rises to her feet.

"Where are you going?" Emory asks, eyebrows knitted.

"I just..." Laura says, not looking back, "I just want to talk to Brett for a bit."

With that, I almost jump to my feet, because the eerily calm tone to her voice implies that she wants to do a little bit more than just talk to Brett, and I need to be there to stop her.

Seconds away from his table, Brett looks up, seeing both Laura and I approaching, Yasmine choosing to stay at the table and grill Emory about his injuries.

"You can be reported for what you did to him, you know." Laura says evenly, eyes calmly boring into Brett as the rest of the table draws their attention to the scene.

"What did I do to him?" Brett asks, tilting his head to the side, feigning ignorance. "You don't have proof for anything."

"Except," I say, mouth pulled into a line, "He has bruises and burn marks?"

"Well," Brett says, eyes lazy and irritatingly supercilious, "He could've been messing around the barbecue. Happens all the time." His eyes harden. "Maybe Emory should've been more careful."

Laura makes a motion towards him, but I tug her back, eyes still firm and dripping with anger.

"Careful," He laughs, and the White Bros™ laugh along with him. "You wouldn't want anything to happen to you."

"Not worth it," I say to Laura as she silently fumes.

"Wouldn't want to... get hurt or go missing." Brett chuckles, grey eyes malicious and emotionless as he rises to his feet, looming over us.

It seems like the next few seconds go in a blur, because the rest of the student body falls into the background, and Laura shoves him, so hard that he falls back to his seat, stumbling backwards.

It's almost like the very foundations of Elkwood shake once her hands come in contact with his chest.

Brett laughs as Laura's chest heaves up and down, and somehow his laugh is more of a threat than any insult. I pat Laura on the back, tugging her back to the table, tempted to give Brett a well-deserved and overdue slap across the face.

However, common sense wins, and Laura falls into step with me, looking back at Brett's table, the foreboding laughter echoing behind us.

***

"It's good that we came here early," Laura says, both of us leaning against our lockers, seated on the carpeted floor, my fingers flying across the keyboard of my laptop as Laura hovers over my screen.

It's been half a week since the Brett Confrontation, and it's safe to say that we've transitioned from being hyper-aware of the concerning smirks that Brett sends our way, to focusing back on Laura's campaign and reaching out to the students. I sneak a glance at Laura from the corner of my eyes. Her features are determined, stance firm, if only slightly rigid.

There's a silent agreement between the two of us to ignore the whole Brett situation and everything that he said at the cafeteria. Brett's ego is far too outstretched, meaning that he's not about to tell the principal that he's been pushed by a girl.

We aren't spending time fueling our anxieties and nerves, or overthinking Brett's every action towards us. After all, he's a manipulator, hellbent on forcing people to second-guess themselves. We can't afford to let him win the mental game.

So instead, we're spending extra time solidifying Laura's likely victory in the upcoming elections. I glance away from the digital campaign poster I'm creating, and I check the time on my phone.

"Students should start arriving now." Laura says, glancing towards the front door.

As if on cue, the doors are pushed in and students start pouring in. I go back to typing across my laptop as Laura accepts greetings from the other kids.

After a few more minutes of typing, I feel a poke in my arm.

"What?" I ask, and Laura points towards the bulletin board, where a throng of students are loitering, murmuring to each other. Some of them glance over to Laura.

"Um..." Yasmine walks over to us, pushing through the mass of students, a nervous look to her eyes, fingers clutching her backpack as her eyes apprehensively touch ours. “Laura, Amina, you two might want to see this.”

That’s all it takes for Laura and I to jump to our feet, speed-walking to the crowd, who parts for us like the Red Sea, allowing us to push through them.

The white piece of paper I see hanging in the center of the bulletin board causes all air to escape my lungs. It reads:

Student: Johnson, Laura

Grade: 10

Expulsion Date: 16 Dec.

Major Offenses include:

- **Physical Aggression**
- **Truancy**
- **Insubordination**

Previous Suspension(s): 2

I can barely formulate a sentence. Yasmine pushes up beside me, turning to Laura. “Is all of this true?” She asks, then insists, “It can’t be, right Laura? Brett could’ve just made this all up.”

Laura doesn't answer, just shakes her head again and again.

"*Laura*," I say, but she backs away, taking slow steps back before whipping around and rushing out of the school, giving me a glimpse of tear streaked cheeks.

I tear the paper from the bulletin board, crumpling it into a small ball, despite the fact that it's already too late.

"Where did you get this?" Yasmine hisses, and I notice she's caught sight of Brett, arms folded and a nauseatingly ugly leer on his lips.

Brett shrugs and responds, "A few weeks ago, I wanted to check if Laura was fit to run," He waves a hand, taking a step forward, "Asked around, checked in with the principal and voiced my concerns." Another shrug. "She let me do a little digging because she had the same concerns." He laughs, hands dug into pockets, "Laura here is a liar and a delinquent." He tilts his head to the side, still smirking, "Someone like her should've never been able to run for president in the first place."

The crowd disperses as Brett leaves, all of them sending contemptuous looks towards Yasmine and I, leaving us alone by the bulletin board.

My fist tightens around the paper and my heart drops to my feet as I glance in the direction that Laura sped off in. This can't be right.

Something about this isn't right.

However, it quickly dawns on me with a startling realization that I don't know much about Laura Johnson.

A fact that might've just caused our chances of victory to dissipate into thin air.

born to sing the blues

My legs swing back and forth in the playground, eyes on the pebbles, feet awkwardly dangling off the swings. Laura's voicemail fills the chilly air for what feels like the hundredth time.

Laura here. If I'm not answering, I'm probably horseback riding or visiting the ranch up north. Kidding. If I'm not answering, I'm probably in a ditch or I just don't want to talk to you. Anyways, you could leave me a message. Might take time to get back to you. I'm crazy busy these days, sorry. Come to think of it, just send me a text.

I did send texts, a couple of which were left on 'read', the majority of which had no indication of Laura seeing them. The wind brushes past my skin, and I shiver, letting the sunset distract me from my phone for a few short minutes.

Everything's in shambles.

I shove my hands into the pockets of my knit sweater. We were *so* close. So close to changing Elkwood for the better, so close to convincing the students that Laura could be the president they needed. Then Brett lit a match, and burned our entire campaign to the ground.

Laura has a history; a history that changes the way the students at Elkwood view her, a history that gives them an excuse to back out of voting for her.

It's hard to imagine the inexplicably casual, future Stu-Co president, eerily calm Laura Johnson to be someone who skipped classes, fought, and broke school property. It doesn't make any sense. What's worse is that Laura won't talk to me, won't clear things up.

There has to be more to the story that she's not telling me. There *has* to be.

"Mina."

The nickname startles me, and my swinging legs come to a stop as my gaze darts to the only person who's ever called me that.

Nat. The orange streetlights trace out his features and he's decked out in a grey jacket, shivering under the cold that he hasn't witnessed for a long time.

"I hate that name, Nat," I say, watching my brother slide onto the swing next to me, shoes digging into the pebbles.

"I know," He says, giving me a tired grin. His eyes flicker up to the stars and he lets out a low chuckle. "Haven't been here in forever."

A quietness sweeps over us, and my hands clutch the chains of my swingset.

"I'm sorry," I say, glancing over to my brother, eyes watery from the rollercoaster of the day.

"No," He says, shaking his head, "*I'm* sorry." Pause. "I mean, I was essentially ditching you. I know how lonely you get here, but I was planning on leaving you behind. It's selfish."

"I just didn't want to say goodbye to my brother," I say, folding my hands onto my laps. "You know, it sucks, not being able to have you visit yearly, but you don't like it here. That's valid, and that's your right."

"But leaving my family behind?" He asks, shaking his head at the ground. "Our whole life we've been taught that the one thing that stays constant is family. If I leave, there's none of that. You'll have to deal with all this crap alone."

"Nat," I say, tilting my head to the side. "I've been braving through all this for years without you."

"I still visited," Nat cuts in, lips pursed.

"True, but that's a couple of holidays a year, the vast majority of it is spent by myself." My voice lowers, "You don't need to feel obligated to come to a place you hate just because of that."

"Don't I?" Nat knits his eyebrows together, a sad smile flitting to his lips. "You know Claudie was crying today?" He asks, and I don't say anything, letting him plow on. "She kept on saying that she'd miss me and that she didn't want me to leave, because I'm supposed to be heading out in a few days. I just sat there, hugging her, and my conscience was just eating at me like hell."

My lips fall into a frown.

Nat runs a hand over his curls. "And it finally dawned on me, you know? Like *holy crap*, I'm not going to see Claudie grow up." A watery laugh escapes his lips. "I won't be there to see her finish elementary school, won't be here to harass her potential crushes." I laugh at that and he continues, "Won't be there to see her graduate high school. I'll miss all her firsts, and it'll destroy me."

"Hey," I say, reaching out to my brother as his shoulders shake.

"All for what?" He leans forward in his swing and almost seems to ask himself, "Not going home because I feel *uncomfortable*? Not seeing my sisters because I don't *like it here*?"

He's reducing all the blatant abuse he deals with in this town—from fellow townspeople—to simple dislike, but it's so much more than that.

He looks at me, brown eyes exhausted and stressed. "And what message am I sending you? That a Davis quits when things get a bit rough?"

"You have your right to your feelings," I say, "we know Davises don't quit. We're all going to be out of here after 12th grade. You endured 12 years of this, like both Claudie and I will."

"And Mom and Dad? What about them? We're gonna leave them here to rot in a retirement home once we've all left and spread out across the country?"

I don't say anything to that.

"I *can't* do that." He runs a hand over his face. "So, no matter what comes up, I've gotta see both you and Claudie through the rest of your childhood, at the very least." He checks his watch, rising to his feet as I mirror his actions.

"You don't have to do that," I say, although my heart swells at his firm promise.

"I feel like I owe that to you, at the very least. I mean, racism and bad weather isn't going to keep me away," He says, his eyes firm. "You ain't about to get rid of me just yet." His eyes glint, crinkling at the sides.

I almost open my mouth to protest, feeling guilty about his change in decision. Before I can, however, I let a long overdue sob escape my throat.

"I'm sorry," My voice shakes, "You don't know how happy that makes me," I say, tears rolling freely as my brother wraps me around in a hug, swaying from side to side.

"We'll visit you, too." I say, my voice muffled into his Supreme hoodie. "Make it easier on all of us."

He pats me on the back, saying, "I'd like that, I really would."

***

The entire family is situated around the living room, seated on varying cushions. Claudie hovers around Nat, latching onto him as though he'll disappear if she lets go, and I sit next to Nat, ice cream in hand as my parents talk from across us.

"Oh," Mom says, setting her ice cream bowl aside and meeting my eyes. "Orion's got his hands full at the diner tomorrow for a big order. His mother's wondering if you could volunteer for just a couple of hours?"

"Is this a request?" I ask, already aware of the answer.

Mom laughs and Dad laughs along with her. "Cute, Amina. Be ready at 4:30 after school. I'll drop you off."

Nat cackles at that, and I make sure to dig my elbow into his side, ignoring the exaggerated yelp that escapes his lips.

"Yes ma'am." I say, raising the spoon to my lips.

"By the way, how's that campaign of yours going?" Dad asks, leaning back against the couch.

"Oh, it's um..." *A major flop.* "We're having a bit of a setback," I say, choosing my words carefully and playing with the strings of my sweatpants.

"Alright," Mom says as Nat narrows his eyes at me from the side.

"And that's with Lauren, no... Lara?" Mom asks, snapping her fingers as she tries to remember, eyes finding the ceiling.

"*Laura*, Mom." I say, and she snaps her fingers once more, nodding at me. "You had *one* job, ma'am," I emphasize, Mom swatting at me from across the table.

"Anyway, invite her over sometime. Seems like a nice girl." Mom says as Dad leans against her side.

"Yeah, I'll..." My heart sinks, "I'll do that." If we ever talk again and manage to fix this mess of things.

"I hope you guys win," Claudie pitches in, letting out a yawn, and I pull her against me with a soft grin.

"Thanks, Clauds," I say as she yawns once more.

"Looks like it's time for someone to head to bed." Nat says, glancing down at Claudie as she gives him a skeptical look.

"Yeah, right," She yawns, curling up into a ball as she usually does when sleep is coming.

A few minutes later, she's knocked out cold. Dad lifts her up, Mom following after him as they head upstairs to her room.

"So, I'm guessing there was a falling out?" Nat asks once they're gone.

I shake my head, letting out an exasperated breath. "Nat, it's a whole mess."

On a day when I didn't appear to be so *drained*, Nat would likely respond to this with: *"oh, a whole mess? As opposed to a quarter of a mess, I presume?"*

To which he would get a cuff in the head, by courtesy of me.

In place of this, Nat hums thoughtfully. "Wanna talk about it?"

I shrug before shaking my head. "No thanks." My phone pings, and I lift it from the floor, noticing four unread messages from Leslie and two from Amber. I sigh, glancing at the screen for a moment before laying it on the floor face-flat.

Noticing Nat's curious eyes, I say, "A lot of pressure to win these elections." Which we're going to lose.

My phone pings at another message. I check the profile, and it reads: EmoryRichards, with a selfie of Emory, his expression seemingly uninterested, brown eyes somewhere far away from the camera.

I purse my lips, realizing he must've gotten my number through Yasmine or Laura, maybe.

"Who's that?" Nat asks, and I give him a look before saying, "The only other black kid in the school."

Nat lets out a burst of incredulous laughter. "Emory Richards? That him?"

"The one and only," I say, holding the screen in front of my face. I swipe through the messages: *It's Emory. Laura isn't answering anyone. Are you going to be by the diner area sometime soon? Tomorrow would be good.*

With Nat's watchful eyes over me, I reply, fingers flying over my phone screen: *yeah, actually,* I find myself typing.

After a few minutes, he responds. *Okay, good. The diner area's a neutral place for everyone so...*

Bubbles appear on the screen, and I wait.

Yasmine is meeting us in that area, too.

I reply with a '*sounds good*', knitting my eyebrows as I type out the question churning in the depths of my mind: *why are we meeting up?*

His next message pops up as Mom and Dad return from downstairs, settling onto the couch as they raise mugs filled with rosemary tea to their lips. Slightly smiling, my eyes flick back down to my screen:

I have a plan to get Laura back into the run. I'm also thinking of teaching Brett a lesson or two.

Pursing my lips, I type out my final question: *do you think this will work?*

Emory's final answer comes briefly and firmly:

Well, we have to give it a shot.

I let out a breath, setting my phone on the coffee table and inhaling deeply.

Then the tiniest shred of hope curls in my chest, eradicating the blue dejection that's been consuming my chest for the entire day.

Because my mind wanders to the possibility of Emory's plan actually working; his plan actually fixing this whole mess, maybe even saving our failing campaign.

I hum.

Maybe we're not so hopeless after all.

the plan

According to Emory, Brett and the White Bros™ drive by the diner every Saturday for hockey practice at the main center.

My phone stays right side up on the kitchen counter as I turn the chicken satay skewers over the grill, Orion glancing at me every so often from the stove.

The scent of spices fills the diner as usual, and although it is usually calming whenever I volunteer here, all I can think about is our impending interaction with Brett, and the series of texts I'm receiving from both Yasmine and Emory.

Of course, the diner's busy and Orion is all over the place, bustling around the kitchen, shooting out orders to everyone else at their stations. He's definitely not going to let me off, not on a night like this. My phone pings again.

Orion lets out a breath as my eyes dart to my phone longingly. "Got somewhere to be?" He asks, and I shake my head at the older boy, eyes still on my phone.

"No."

"Doesn't look like it," He says as I glance over at the array of notifications on my home screen.

"It's stupid," I say, still turning the skewers, "I kinda have this campaign thing, and it's at a bad place right now. My friends and I are trying to see how we can fix everything."

"Okay," Orion says, knitting his eyebrows at me as he inspects one of the people cooking, "I don't really remember asking, though."

I give him a look, and his face remains passive, with the exception of an almost imperceptible twitch in his lips.

"You're mean," I say, as Orion's lips twitch once more.

"Finish with the satays," He says, nodding towards my grill, and I let my shoulders sag because at this moment, Emory and Yasmine feel like they're miles out of reach.

When I've finished turning the last skewer, I turn to the sink that's piled with dishes. Water starts running when I open the tap, and I start to get to work.

"What are you doing?" Orion asks from across the kitchen, causing my head to snap up.

"Working," I deadpan, eyes dull.

"Hey, I said you should finish the satays." Orion says, eyebrows raised.

"Which I did," I say, slowly. We stare at each other for a few moments, Orion's eyes wide and dark as though he's giving me a silent message.

"Wait," I start, trying to quash the miniscule bit of hope rising to my chest.

He juts his head towards the door. "Go on."

"Orion—" I start, eyes scouting the entire kitchen where everyone's hard at work.

"We'll manage."

I still pause, lips parted as I try to decipher whether or not he's messing with me.

"Get out of here," He says, and once it clicks, I grab my phone, tug my apron off, and rush through the doors, giving Orion the most grateful smile I can muster. "Thank you."

Orion just nods, turning back to supervise one of the teenagers washing the dishes.

In seconds, I'm outside of the door, scrolling through my messages. Messages from Emory that read: *We're just across the block from the diner. Okay, we're waiting near the chinatown. Hurry up.*

My Air Force Ones pad on the pavement quickly, phone in hand as I scroll through the messages.

With a quick response, I walk down the block, eyes scouting the entire area and the bustling streets of downtown, the working people with their coffees in one hand and phones in the other, the loud honking of cars, the chilly gusts of air.

Then I see them. All three of them, Yasmine waving me over eagerly as I rush over to them. The air escapes from my lips in white gusts and soon I'm in front of them, eyes meeting each of theirs.

Laura hesitantly drags her gaze from the floor, meeting my eyes, hands shoved into jacket pockets as the wind billows her dark waves.

"I've got a lot to tell you." She says, adjusting the patterned coat, and my eyes soften at that, although my stance remains rigid.

She lets out a breath. "I'm about to explain everything."

***

"My dad has cancer."

When the four words leave Laura's lips, silence consumes the entire bench. I'm seated next to Yasmine, Laura across from us and Emory leaning against the side of the bench, eyes unreadable.

"Put a lot of stress on my mom and I back when I was still enrolled in my old school." Pause. "He was in and out of the hospital, and we spent a lot of time there."

Yasmine takes a deep breath, mouth opening and closing as if to ask a question.

"He's fine, as of now. Well, better." Laura cuts in, "The chemotherapy is working. Back then, it was terrible. His health was constantly fluctuating. It was turbulent."

"I'm sorry," I say, not knowing what else to say as my eyes gently find Laura's, causing her to wave a hand.

"I'm not going to use my dad as an excuse to justify everything in the report you saw." She leans forward. "The truancy, though? That wasn't me skipping school to go shopping or whatever; that was actually me constantly visiting the hospital." She lets out a dry chuckle, eyes finding the pale sky. "I had this irrational fear that if I left him alone in the hospital, he would..."

No one finishes the sentence.

Discomfort arises in my stomach, consuming my insides as I try not to think about the word she was about to say.

Her fear isn't as irrational as she thinks, either. From the looks of it, he was barely hanging onto life.

I wouldn't leave his side, either.

"And they recorded the absences as unexcused?" Emory asks, sneakers digging into the light snow.

"Yeah. My mom usually emailed to let them know, but sometimes she forgot with everything that was going on. And some emails didn't receive responses."

"As for the *insubordination*," Laura continues, leaning on the heels of her feet. "I questioned everything, and the administration didn't like that." Laura says with a shrug. "I wanted *more*. And they didn't want to give me that. They'd steer me towards easy classes, unadvanced classes." She clasps her hands together. "I put my foot down, because I was just as qualified as any of the other students there. Oakwood wouldn't give me that, and I made sure to push back. They called me pushing back insubordination."

Laura trills her lips. "There was one day that a girl in my class called me a word. Something I'm not going to repeat."

Emory sucks in a breath, tilting his head to the side. "That bad, huh?"

Laura meets his eyes. "Worse." She bites her bottom lip. "And it wasn't a new thing. She'd constantly been making my life hell there, saying stupid crap about my dad."

My fists tighten into balls, anxiety swirling in my mind as I think of this *girl*, and how low anyone could be to use someone's *sick dad* to insult them.

"I eventually lost it, yelled at her." A pause, then a wry laugh. "She claimed I attacked her, and Oakwood put that incident on my record as *physical aggression*."

"That sucks," Yasmine says, shaking her head.

"Oakwood kept eagle eyes on me, too." She runs a hand through her hair. "Any misstep would be punished. Any remark I made towards any of the blatant racists at the school—staff included—would be etched into my permanent record." She pauses, tracing a dangling earring. "The racists?" She sends us a cynical half-grin. "They walked free. And their permanent records? Immaculate."

"Your parents didn't...?" I ask, eyes rising to hers from my cuffed jeans.

"My mom sent a full-length email," Laura laughs, "She explained the bullying, the racist comments... Oakwood never responded. When confronted, they said they never received it."

My lips part, my head shaking back and forth.

"That's messed up." Emory says, kicking at the snow coating the sidewalk.

"I mean," Laura shrugs, "Oakwood hated my guts. The teachers expected me to be rebellious, to be a bad kid. Any misstep would prove that. After all, if you look for something, you'll see it. Even if it's not there."

Yasmine nods, and Laura continues, " I think I'll always stand by the notion that I was getting pushed out of Oakwood since the day I stepped foot in the building." Pursed lips. "The place wrecked me." Emory's eyebrows fly upwards as Laura's features remain unreadable. "Dad being sick was an extra stressor." Her voice is smooth, calm even, despite the fact that none of what she's telling us is particularly light. "What's done is done," She finishes, rubbing her temples. "I can't sit down here and tell you I'm perfect, but I also can't sit by and let you think that some stupid piece of paper says anything about me." An exhale is drawn from her lips. "Unfortunately, there's no going back now."

Wind dances through the air, racing through our hair and clothing. The sound of the gusts dominate the silence until I speak up.

"I'm sorry," I say, feeling my eyes soften.

Laura trills her lips again. "Don't apologize," She says. "This is between me and Oakwood."

"Are you still alright?" I ask, carefully, Laura tugging the corner of her lips upwards, if only slightly.

"Yeah," Laura shrugs. "I'm getting over it. I've finished. I've left. I'm trying to turn the page." She lets out a breath. "I want to forget that hell." Pause. "Still want to apologize to all of you, though."

Emory hums, glancing down at her, his hands still slipped into the pockets of his dark sweatpants.

She runs a hand through her hair, "I thought I could leave Oakwood's damage behind." An exhale. "I'm sorry I didn't tell you guys about it before it got out." She bites her bottom lip. "You really shouldn't have heard it from Brett of all people." A dry laugh. "Unfortunately, a sheet full of complaints won't tell you the full story." A pause. "Any story, really."

Yasmine leans forward, hand ghosting over Laura's shoulder. "Don't worry about it," she says, and I nod along with her, Emory shooting Laura a half grin.

Oakwood wrought hell in Laura's life. She speaks simply, but the weight of her words outweigh the careful movement of her lips. A school in which she was constantly treading over glass. One stutter, one slip, and the glass shattered. In Oakwood, Laura didn't *get* to make mistakes, only recorded offences.

Not only that, but a lot of the alleged offences against her were blatant lies.

"Brett did that because he saw you as a threat," I find myself saying. "If he really thought that you were unfit to be president, he would have done it earlier on."

"Or he probably wouldn't have bothered digging you up in the first place, because he wouldn't feel the need to find dirt on you." Emory cuts in, letting his shoulders relax into a shrug.

Laura lets out a breath, raising her hands to the air. "Luckily, I've paid way more than my dues already."

A smirk curves onto Emory's lips at that. "That's good, but we have one more person that hasn't paid his dues yet."

A glint appears in Laura's dark eyes, and the rest of us mirror the look.

"That's right," She replies, eyes still glinting, "Brett better be ready for us."

white bros™ headquarters

The hockey rink is essentially White Bros™ headquarters. As in, it's jam packed with the army, which consists of Brett, his friends, and other future frat boys from other schools.

They cut through the rink, skates scraping the ice, hockey sticks fighting hungrily for the puck.

Nat used to play hockey before he quit, but he played long enough for me to recognize every play in the game, every bad move, every split second decision that should've been made.

"Do you have... any idea what's happening right now?" Yasmine whispers from next to me as we all stand aligned by the stands, a little ways away from the parents.

"Strangely enough, yeah." I whisper back to her before I lean forward, lips twitching at a backhand shot.

"Got that one in pretty well," Laura hums at one of the plays made on the ice.

Emory shakes his head. "Maybe, or maybe the goalie's just a sieve."

"Isn't Brett the goalie?" Yasmine asks, amusement curving onto her lips as pink from the cold tinges her cheeks.

"To be honest, I can't tell. Don't know what his number is." Laura replies, turning to Emory.

"I'm pretty sure he's number 6," Emory replies, "And yeah, that'd make him the goalie."

Laughter escapes our lips and the nearby parents send us wary glances, causing us to haltingly slow our laughter and bring our attention back to the scrimmage on the rink.

Soon, the coach calls all the players to the center, shouting out some pieces of feedback before telling them to get off the ice.

So, they do. They skate up to the stands, heavy skates clinking against the ground. Within the throng of boys, one of them removes a black helmet, letting light brown hair fall free. Then his eyes trace the entire area before they land on us.

He squints, nudging one of the lackeys next to him and laughing. Then he trudges over to us, standing just a few feet away from our little group.

"Do I need to file a restraining order, Johnson?" Brett asks, grin smug as ever as he turns his gaze to Laura, who straightens up, unwavering.

"No offense, but this is a delinquent-free zone," The redhead next to him says. "We don't need any trouble here."

"Ironic," Laura replies, utterly unfazed. "You're talking about filing a restraining order on me when Emory here has every reason to report *you.*"

"Oh, you're still hung up on that?" Brett rolls his neck, eyes glazing over in boredom.

"On you attempting to give me third-degree burns because you're a sadist?" Emory asks with a cold laugh. "Because, yeah, a lil bit."

"Oh, did we hurt you, princess?" Brett coos, jutting out his bottom lip as the surrounding hockey players watch eagerly.

"Nah," Emory shrugs, "just irritated me." He says, elbows resting on the stand as he leans backwards.

"Want us to kiss the burns better?" A freckle-faced one asks, holding a hand to his chest.

"That'll be unnecessary," Yasmine says, fingers entangled. "I think we'll just go with reporting."

"Yeah, you do that." Brett says, letting out a smug gust of air. "You don't have *any proof whatsoever*, but you do that, Abadi."

"Really?" I ask, tucking a braid behind my ear as Laura hums.

Emory leans back against the stands, tilting his head to the side. "You realize you have a history right? Like you've skipped school, disrespected teachers, smoked on and off school grounds?"

"Dude, none of that is on my record," Brett laughs, arms folded. "*Again*, there's no evidence."

"You actually got away with doing all that?" Laura asks, arms folded to match his, as she catches my eyes for a moment, giving me a nearly imperceptible nod.

Brett laughs. "Who do you think gets the vapes into school?" He gets a somewhat aggressive clap on the back from the guy next to him. "Missed an entire day to head over to the skate park." A wink. "As far as Ms. Anderson knows, I was sick with the flu." A pause. "I clean up my tracks," He shrugs, "you could learn a thing or two about it, expellee." His eyes cut into Laura as he says this.

"You don't know anything about what happened," She says, fists slowly clenching as Yasmine gently rubs a circle onto her shoulder.

"Great," Brett shrugs, "Because, frankly, I don't really care, but, listen." He lowers his voice. "I can do whatever the hell I want around here. Emory had what was coming to him." He shrugs, shooting daggers at Emory who returns the look with even more gusto. Brett winks. "It was fun, by the way."

Laughs slide from their lips, frostier than the chilly air of the skating rink.

"Just get the hell out of here." Brett laughs again. "Unless you'd like to be escorted out. In fact, we can do that for you personally,

Emory." His eyes scope the rest of us as Emory lets out something resembling a scoff at the comment.

Brett plows on. "That includes the rest of you."

"We're not obligated to leave just because you said so," my voice comes out firm, eyes steady, stance solid.

"Okay," Brett laughs, his followers laughing along with him. "Stay as long as you want, and, you know, you can say *whatever* you want for all I care. You know as well as we do that you're just wasting your time."

"That's where you're wrong," Emory says lightly, amusement dripping from his tone as he nods his head towards me before his eyes return to Brett. "Little bit smarter than we let on."

I hold up my phone, video still playing and a grin tugging at my lips as the seconds go by.

"Footage is pretty solid evidence," Laura tilts her head to the side. "You'll be hard pressed trying to talk your way out of this one." A sly grin curves onto her lips as she nods towards my phone.

Brett pales and the sight is almost comical.

"What?" He asks, taking a step forward, reaching from my phone. I step back from him, holding my phone out of reach.

"Don't do that," he says, eyes widened, lips parted.

"Why not?" Yasmine bats her eyelashes, "You've got the presidential elections in the bag, haven't you?"

Brett bites his bottom lip, roughly, moving towards us as we step out of reach. "You better delete that crap." His eyes cut into mine.

"No thanks," I send him a honey sweet smile in response. "I'll be keeping this footage."

"You don't need to worry about it," Laura juts out her bottom lip. "No one's going to believe us, you said so yourself."

"Get rid of the *damn* video," Brett says, face reddening.

"Nah, man." Emory smirks, tilting his head to the side. "Best luck on the elections, though." He whispers, tauntingly. "You'll need it."

"You're not going to screw this up for me," Brett says, voice dripping in venom.

"Don't worry." Laura says with a pout. "You already did that yourself."

That's all it takes for Brett to snap.

He lunges for me, and my heart palpitates as I jump out of his reach, causing him to stumble.

The rest of his troop jumps into action, movements clunky and restrained in their heavy skates, making it easy for us to weave around them.

Laura's eyes sparkle at their pathetic attempts to grab us.

"Run!" I yell, and the rest of us exchange amused, adrenaline-filled glances before speeding out of the area.

Brett and his group start kicking off their skates onto the solid ground, some sliding sneakers onto their feet as we start zipping through the skating rink.

We push through the double doors, running out onto the pavement and sprinting down the sidewalk. Yasmine lets out a series of curses as the heavy padding of running shoes come from behind us. A glance back reveals Brett and four-or-so of his lackeys, all of them jogging after us.

Emory lets out a string of curses, looking back at the running boys to give them smug looks paired with indecent facial expressions and gestures.

"*God*, Emory," Laura laughs, still running at my side, "stop triggering them."

"A bit too late for that," Yasmine huffs as we turn a corner, the boys yelling out obscenities from behind us.

"Where exactly are we supposed to go?" Laura pants, glancing back every few seconds as we jog to the end of the street and midway onto the next block.

This. I think while my breaths come out in quick gusts. *This* is why I hate track with a burning passion.

The adrenaline is dwindling, and they're going to catch up with us at some point. Suddenly, a bulb flickers on in my mind.

"Guys," I say, looking over at my acquaintances—friends—that are still breathing heavily, chests rising and falling. "I know where to go."

"Thank God," Yasmine says, and I gesture towards them to follow me.

I zip back in the direction we're coming from, so we're right across from Brett's group.

Emory glances over at me, eyebrows raised as if to ask: *this is your life-saving plan?*

I take a sharp left, the group stumbling after me as I swing into a familiar restaurant, pushing through the doors and panting as the everyday customers gape at me.

Then shouts of exclamation break out of their voices, all in various languages, Ms. Cruz's exclamation of shock cutting through the cacophony of dialects.

"Why are you running?" Mr. Asfour stares blankly at us, rounded glasses sliding onto the bridge of his nose. I can't help but let out a painfully exhausted laugh.

"More importantly, *who* are you running from?" Miss Silva asks, hand running through her short curls as she takes us in.

Orion makes his way to the front, eyes traveling over our wind-blown and sweaty selves. He opens his mouth as if to ask something, but he's cut off by a pounding on the door.

"He's lost it," Yasmine mutters, as Brett glares through the glass, his teammates a little ways away from him. Orion rolls his eyes, pushing past us and opening the door.

"What are you doing here?" He asks, boredly, the door shutting behind him and drowning out the rest of the conversation.

Our eyes stay on the glass as Brett tries to look over Orion's shoulder, pointing at the doors. Orion shakes his head, causing Brett to step up to him as if to intimidate him. Although, once he takes in Orion's 6' 1", he takes a step back. Orion mouths something else and Brett's eyes find us through the glass. I wiggle my fingers in a wave at him as Laura blows a taunting kiss.

His fingers clench before Orion says something else to him. Then, with one glance back at us, he spits onto the ground, shuffling off with the rest of his lackeys.

Orion brushes his apron, returning to the shop, shutting the door behind him.

"What did you say to him?" I ask, eyes trailing over to the empty sidewalk where Brett and the White Bros™ were standing just seconds before.

Orion waves a dismissive hand. "Just told him that he can't come in without a reservation. Brought the police into the conversation when he wouldn't leave."

"You lied?" I ask, my lips twitching in amusement. Because the idea of *Orion Henderson* calling the police is absurd to me. He'd sooner jump off a moving train, I'm sure.

"Stretched the truth a little bit. You're welcome." Orion says, making his way down to the kitchen in his usual gait.

A half smile curves onto my lips. Although, I doubt Brett would be all that scared of a 911 call. I'm still betting it was Orion's imposing build that caused them to get out of the place as fast as they did.

From behind me, Yasmine, Laura, and Emory utter a quick '*thank you*', eyes finding Orion as he shrugs them off. The customers return to eating their dishes, attention drawn away from the four of us now that everything is seemingly resolved.

A few seconds pass before Orion comes to a halt at the door, spinning around so that he's facing us.

"Well, get over here." He says, beckoning towards us. "You're all here, and we need more hands in the kitchen."

With quick glances exchanged between the four of us, we rush towards him, elated laughter filling the air, because for the first time, it feels like we've won.

Really won, even if it's only for a second.

brett gets exposed

"*And*... sent." With one last tap, Emory leans backwards in his seat, eyeing his laptop, hands positioned behind his head.

The juicery's mellow music rings in the background, and Yasmine nods, eyes still on her phone as Laura's eyes scope the laptop.

"So, what's the plan?" Laura asks, from across the round, neon-green table, hands clasped.

"Well, I emailed the video to the principal, so I guess she'll decide what's going to happen to Brett after he's fessed up to everything. I also anonymously submitted it onto the school blog, so people should see it in seconds."

"And the elections?" I ask, eyes finding Laura's as I hold my smoothie cup between my hands.

Yasmine hums, opening her mouth to pitch in when the usual jingle of the juicery chimes ring throughout the space, drawing all attention to the entrance.

Amber Wesley is standing at the front, arms folded, lips twitching when her gaze finds us.

"She's coming our way," Emory mutters in a sing-song voice, eyes narrowed as he eyes the dirty blonde who comes to a halt at our table.

"I can't believe this," Amber says, grin widening as she slides into a spare seat at our table.

"Can't believe what?" Laura asks, stirring her mango smoothie with a straw.

Amber holds up her glossy phone screen. Squinting, I see Brett, hockey jersey glinting underneath the lights, eyes angry as he stares directly into the camera.

"This just got submitted onto the school blog." Amber says, shaking her phone screen, Brett's angry words cutting through the audio.

"His campaign is over," Amber emphasizes, hair falling over to the side, hands running through her waves. "It *has* to be."

Yasmine clears her throat, and Amber's head snaps up from her phone, raising a hand to her chest to quickly muster fake sympathy.

"I am *so* sorry about what happened to you, Emory." Amber says, holding her phone to her chest, her green eyes dripping with faux emotion.

Emory coughs, a badly-concealed laugh peeking out from his tone. "Well, things happen."

So, you had no idea?" Yasmine asks, tilting her head to the side as Laura narrows her eyes at Amber.

Amber shrugs, muttering quickly. "I mean, someone mentioned something at the table, but I didn't really catch on to it."

"What?" Laura asks, and Emory blinks rapidly. Like that one blinking white guy gif. I'd laugh if Amber's statement wasn't so ridiculously unfunny. Any laughter I might have falls dead in my throat and dies there. Like a shriveled butterfly crushed underfoot.

"Well, I thought it'd be better to get the full story." Amber attempts to amend, making everything a million times worse.

"What full story?" The question slips out of my lips in a second. It's tentative, but the confusion is still hanging from my tone.

Someone got physically attacked by a group of cowards, without any provocation. The *full story*?

All Brett did was confirm what we already knew. He physically attacked someone without provocation. Not like provocation would justify what happened, anyway.

The thing that makes my blood run cold is the fact that *Amber knew.* Amber knew the entire time, had the information secured in the back of her mind. She *chose* to brush it away, chose to ignore it until it was convenient for her.

Amber's eyes land on the ceiling, leaning back against her seat, arms sliding over her chest, gaze unimpressed, dripping with some patronization. "The full story, okay? All parts of what happened. Not just what Emory claims happened." A glance towards Emory, a toffee-sweet smile. "No offense."

A beat, before Laura hums. "What do you mean?" An innocent question, before she troughs on. "It seems like you were aware of it, but *chose* to ignore it." Her eyebrows are scrunched as she stirs her smoothie.

After all, had she really wanted the full story, she would have researched, looked into it. *"The full story"* is some lousy excuse for bystanding. Always has been, always will be.

Makes me sick.

Pink tinges at Amber's cheeks as she opens her mouth to shoot out an indignant reply.

"That's what it sounded like," Yasmine clarifies, eyebrows perfectly arched.

"Yeah, well," Emory cuts in, giving Amber a wry grin. "That's the full story. Thanks for the sympathy. It's over and done." He claps his hands together. "Thanks for dropping by."

"Just here to check in," Amber says, smoothing down her skirt. When no one else makes a move to say anything else, she speaks up again. "Well, anyways." She turns to Laura, "You've got this election guaranteed. Most importantly, Brett is finally getting exposed for the fraud he is."

Emory and I exchange glances, and Yasmine coughs. Laura, however, maintains a poker face, ever-the-politician. The irony of Amber's statement causes me to poke a tongue in my cheek.

I mean, Amber cyberbullied Millie, yet launched her campaign as if she was against bullying. In fact, one of the slogans still rings in my head: *Amber Wesley to make Elkwood a more inclusive space.* Not to mention the complete 180° she did with Brett. One day, she was kissing his feet. The next, she was enlisting us to take him down.

"Things are definitely changing around here." I finally say, a half smile rising to my lips.

"Definitely," Amber agrees, rising from the table. "Anyways, I've got to go." She leaves the chair untucked as she takes a few steps away, before calling over her shoulder. "Good luck." Then, she giggles. "Not like there's any more competition."

She stops by the counter, placing money forward, and grabbing a cup, taking a generous swig out of the drink as the door shuts behind her.

When she's gone, Yasmine purses her lips. "Well, that was... interesting."

"It's like she's out for Brett's blood." I say, brushing my thumb over my bottom lip.

"Which is ironic," Emory adds, leaning back in his chair, "seeing as just a few weeks ago, she was completely sucking up to him."

Laura claps her hands together. "I'm guessing I have her vote?"

Yasmine bites her bottom lip, staring after the exit. "I'm guessing you do."

"Which wouldn't matter anyway," Emory says, "because half of the original candidates won't be running."

"You're certain that Brett will drop out of the race?" I ask, tilting my head to the side.

Laura snorts. "He's not about to drop out, but he'll definitely be kicked out."

"So, it's you and Walt." Yasmine murmurs, resting her chin on her fist.

"The student body is just gonna have to choose between the lesser of two evils." Emory shrugs, his lips twitching slightly.

Laura shoves him to the side, almost instantaneously and he shoots a show-stopping grin, dripping with amusement.

"That wasn't very cash money of you," I state, eliciting laughter from Yasmine who's seated next to me.

"I'm kidding." Emory laughs, taking a slurp of his juice, giving Laura a firm nod. "The elections are yours."

"Well, time to see what the school says, come Monday." Laura nods slowly, eying each of us knowingly, and we all mirror the look, because once Monday comes, judgement day comes.

***

Monday morning, I'm seated in the office, Laura next to me. Class starts in just under 10 minutes, and the principal—Ms. Anderson— eyes the two of us from underneath her horn-rimmed glasses.

No sooner had Laura and I stepped foot in the school—earlier this morning—had Ms. Anderson ushered us to her headquarters, catching our eyes and leading us to the most despised room in Elkwood.

Her office.

Ms. Anderson's room is plain. The center consists of a black chair behind a mahogany desk. Pictures of her and a balding man are placed on varying parts of the walls. An empty glass vase is positioned towards the corner of her desk, intricate designs crawling up the object. Finally, a plain silver laptop sits atop her desk. Everything in the room is stiff, not unlike the navy pantsuit the principal is wearing, a red blouse peeking from the blazer, emphasizing cherry red lips and cold, narrowed eyes.

"So, yesterday, I received footage from Emory Richards." Ms. Anderson says, adjusting the collar of her blazer. "Brett M. was depicted in this video." Pause. "I'd be talking to Emory right now, but it appears that he has a conflicting appointment this morning."

"It's a doctor's appointment," Laura says, raising a hand. Her expression is passive, almost emotionless. He's supposed to get medications for his burns.

I purse my lips. Brett's claim about Ms. Anderson doubting Laura's eligibility for StuCo president is undoubtedly the cause of Laura's heightened level of indifference, with her passiveness straying into standoffish territory.

Ms. Anderson rests her arms on the back of her office chair, staring us down. “Well, the next time you see him, let him know that I’d like to meet with him.”

Silence. Laura and I slowly nod, letting the quietness consume the small room.

“So, uh,” I exchange glances with Laura, her dark eyes shining underneath the bright lights. “What about Brett?”

“What *about* Brett?” Ms. Anderson asks, leaning forward behind her chair, eyes cutting into mine.

“He admitted to physically attacking another student.” Laura says, eyebrows raised and knitted together.

“On the clip.” Ms. Anderson challenges. “I have no idea what went on before and after the video. He could’ve been prodded, the footage could’ve been manipulated.”

“By who?” Laura asks, eyes narrowed, letting out a slightly venomous chuckle.

Ms. Anderson tilts her head to the side, eyeing Laura in an equally venomous manner. “I just don’t know, Laura.”

She's inferring something; something she won't put to words, but the meaning behind her vague statement is crystal clear.

"Ms. Anderson, I—" I start, eyes finding hers, but Laura rises to her feet, cool demeanor diminishing.

"You don't know, Ms. Anderson?" Laura asks, tone smooth as honey but eyes icy. "Because the footage seems awfully clear to me."

"Well," Ms. Anderson says, adjusting her glasses, the faintest arrogance creeping onto her lips. "I'll have to talk to Brett first. See what he thinks."

"The footage kind of already illustrates what he thinks, though." I say, eyes squinting, pulling my bottom lip beneath my teeth.

"Exactly. The footage reveals everything you need to know," The honey is slowly falling from Laura's tone and giving way to ice. "It's concrete evidence."

"We'll see, Miss Johnson." Ms. Anderson replies, evenly. Laura makes a move to say something, but Ms. Anderson raises her hand.

"To me," Ms. Anderson says, eyes drifting over me. "It looks like you're just looking to eliminate your competition, instead of working hard like the other candidates."

Laura's mouth parts, before she lets out a cold, dry laugh almost readying herself to shoot something back. With that, I kick her leg from underneath the table, Laura letting out a heavy breath.

Ms. Anderson smiles, slowly. We're at an impasse. One word, and we're out of this school. There's no way to go from here, and every one in the room is painfully aware of that.

"You're dismissed, ladies." Ms. Anderson says.

She's not going to do anything about the incident. The fact is painfully clear. Talking to Brett is just a deflection, something that won't end with any results.

With one tug of Laura's arm, I pull her towards the door, stepping out of the frame as the door shuts behind us.

Laura laughs, but it's devoid of any mirth. Frustration takes the form of angry watery eyes. "This is Oakwood all over again."

"I'm sure we're still going to win," I say, uncertainness dripping from my voice.

"It's not even about that," Laura says, whipping around to meet my eyes. Her eyes are frustrated, cheeks tinged with pink. "It's about the fact that Emory Richards was assaulted and burned by these *psychopaths*, and nothing is going to happen to them." She falls back against the lockers with a thud. "He's not going to get justice."

"It happens." I say, and the words sound dead, even to myself. After all, what will people say? *Maybe the kid shouldn't have gone to the barbecue in the first place. Maybe he should've chosen better friends. Maybe it was an accident. Maybe there's more to the story. Maybe he said something to them.*

No one will ever look at the real issue, which is the fact that Brett and his group assaulted Emory. No one will ever emphasize that what happened was unjustifiable under any circumstances. No one will realize that Emory did nothing wrong, that really, he was the victim.

No one will care.

"No, we can't just say that." Laura says, fists clenching. "If Emory doesn't get justice, it'll go against everything my campaign is standing for." A watery, angry laugh escapes her lips. "Everything *I'm* standing for."

She sinks down to the bottom of the lockers, and I sink down next to her, legs pulled to my chest.

I sigh, looking over to her. "What do you suggest, then?"

"You tell me," Laura says, glancing over at me, dark hair pressed against the lockers.

I tilt my head to the side. What have people always done when the ruling party was unfair to them?

There's the cry of the unheard, something that rumbles in the background, present but ignored.

It's how unheard voices have always been heard— a collective storm of rebellion that *rattles* the earth, a united front that grabs the broken system by the shoulders and shakes it, forcing those in power to *see* us.

Fire appears in my eyes, and I turn over to Laura, a grin appearing on my lips. "We're going to protest."

elkwood has an issue

Rap has been blasting from the speakers for hours on end. The dining room is bustling, each member of the family situated at different ends of the table.

Claudette sits across from me, taking spoonfuls of soup as she belts out the lyrics, giggling whenever a taboo word is bleeped from the speakers. Whenever the n-word comes up, a hum travels through the family, an awkward gap appearing as we continue with the rest of the lyrics.

Too many bad memories, after all.

Claudie's especially into it, making vivid arm movements as she jives, eliciting laughs from the rest of the family.

After a few more minutes of nods, lyrics and the clink of spoons against bowls, Dad lowers the volume of his speaker.

"Time to chat." He says, eyes traveling over Nat, Claudie, and I. "My three kids, all here in one space."

Mom shakes her head with a grin. "Doesn't happen very often these days."

"What's everyone been up to lately?" Dad asks, hands clasping over the table.

"Volunteering," Nat says, the halo practically hovering over his head.

Claudie waves a hand in the air. "Learning about the fifty states." She chirps.

My parents nod, before turning to me, Mom's hand tracing over a silver necklace. "Amina?"

Let's see. Launching a campaign, winning over the student body, trying to take down Brett McSomething, attempting to start a school-wide protest.

"You were working on that campaign, weren't you?" Dad asks, jutting a spoon in my direction.

"Where are you with it now?" Nat asks, as Claudie looks over at me, taking slow slurps of her soup.

Any other day, I probably would've said something vague about the progress and whatnot. The truth is that this whole thing has evolved into so much more than some dumb bid for presidency. Now, it's about shaking the very foundations of Elkwood.

"I'm organizing a protest." I blurt, causing all eyes around the table to widen.

"Sorry, what?" Dad asks.

"A protest." I repeat slowly.

"They're going to hate this," Mom says, tilting her head to the side. *They* being Elkwood: the whole community, the neighborhood, the school. Maybe even the town.

"I know, I just..." I shake my head for a second, fingers running through dark braids. I meet my parents' eyes, and the whole story spills out. Emory having parts of his flesh seared off by Brett and his friends, Brett cockily fessing up to doing it, Ms. Anderson brushing the whole case aside with a passive aggressive grin to put salt on the wound.

"That could be classified as a hate crime, right Deb?" Dad asks, turning to Mom, who purses her lips in thought, no doubt mentally searching into her knowledge of law that resides in her mind.

"And he just... followed them to their barbecue?" Nat asks, leaning back in his seat, eyebrows raised.

"Hindsight is 20/20," I say, halfheartedly, lips pursed.

"Maybe it's just me, but I wouldn't be heading to the park, unsupervised, with, uh, *racists*." Nat replies, eyebrows raised.

"Isn't that against the law?" Claudie asks, piping up. "To set a boy on fire?" Pause. "On purpose?"

"Yeah," Mom hums, nodding as Claudie's eyes widen almost comically.

"And Ms. Anderson is just letting it slide?" Dad asks, slight lines curving into his face as he frowns. *Not surprised*, I think, *just disappointed.*

"Hence the reason we're protesting," I say, letting out a breath.

Silence crosses the table.

I raise my head, my voice slightly shaky, "You're not going to talk me out of it?" I ask.

Dad chuckles, one eyebrow quirked. "Why would we do that?"

"I dunno," I reply, exhaling. "Because I should be keeping things toned down?"

"I mean, Emory Richards was *attacked*?" Mom asks with slight incredulousness, clinking her glass back onto the table. "And Elkwood's administration is about to brush it under the *rug*?"

"Like the Rosewood Massacre." Dad coughs.

Mom trills her lips as Nat cuts in, glancing towards me. "I mean, peaceful assembly is your fundamental right. At *this* point?" He shakes his head. "I can't say I wouldn't consider doing the same thing."

"You know, your grandma actually protested back in '65." Dad nods, raising a glass to his lips. "Smack in the middle of the civil rights movement. Barely a few decades ago."

"*What*? Like with Martin Luther King!?" Claudie nearly cries out, rising to her feet.

"Yes, Claudie," Mom says, waving a hand to gesture for my sister to sit down. "She was part of the sit-ins, almost every single day."

Nat raises a hand. "At seventeen she was part of the Children's Crusade in Birmingham. She told me that herself."

"Know what happened to those kids?" Dad asks with one of those sad smiles tugging at his lips. I shake my head despite the fact that I know this story well. Dad continues, "they got hosed down, maced, attacked, had dogs set on them." Dad adds. "Children as young as *six.*"

"Because they wanted equality." Mom says, a rueful smile sliding onto her lips. "Nothing more, nothing less."

"Did Grandma meet MLK, though?" Claudie asks, now back on her seat but still practically shaking with excitement. *Girl has priorities.*

"Don't know whether she ever came face-to-face with him," Dad says, pursing his lips.

"Oh," Claudie says, mirroring his look. Nat nudges her and she grins, eyes brightening. "Still *so* cool, though."

Mom lets out a little laugh at Claudie's excitement, turning towards me. "We can help you out with the protest," She says, leaning forward in her seat, "we can see how you're planning it out, try and work out details, make sure everything stays safe."

"Grandma will be through the roof about the whole thing." Nat adds, a half grin appearing on his lips.

"We'll call her," Dad waves a hand, "Talk to her, get some advice, try to be strategic about it. We need to be extremely careful and cautious. We'll also have *guidelines* and supervision."

"So, this is... this is actually happening," I murmur, almost more to myself than anyone else.

Mom reaches forward, grabbing onto my hand as fiery yet motherly eyes meet mine. "It's happening, baby."

***

I scribble the last letter, capping my pen and placing it to the side. I shift the poster over to Laura, who holds it in front of her, pursing her lips.

The library's quiet as usual, olives and browns decorating the space and Yasmine peers over Laura's shoulder, eyes roving over the poster as Emory leans back against his cushion, fingers brushing over a white bandage on the side of his face.

One of many.

"I don't know about this," Emory says, leaning back against his cushion and sinking into it.

Our eyes travel over to him and he glances back at us, hands clasped. "I mean," he continues, "I'm getting treated for the burns, anyway. They're going to find a way to villainize this whole thing," He waves a hand. "And we're all going to be here for at least two more years. At least, I will. *I think*." He raises a hand to his chest. "And I don't need Brett on me for the rest of my time here."

Yasmine hums, twirling the marker in her hand absentmindedly.

"*One* incident. They'll claim it was an accident and then the whole thing will be pointless." He slides his hands through dark curls. "It's *one* incident. Who gives a crap?"

Silence. Pensive, thought-whirring silence.

"But, that's the thing," I find myself saying, meeting Emory's eyes. "It's not just that *one* thing." I pause before pressing on. "It's about so many things." Pause. "It's about Ms. Wilson trying to lighten up slavery."

Laura raises a hand, nodding. "And listing the supposed 'pros and advantages to all' in colonization." People were *massacred*. That type of statement makes me feel all types of nauseous.

It's about the glares the staff send me every time I walk past them.

"It's about Max Wright harassing me about *suicide bombers* in freshman year, and barely getting a slap on the wrist in return." Yasmine says, fists trembling.

It's about the fact that *To Kill A Mockingbird* has never characterized the black characters.

It's about the fact that Miss Daniels was angry at me when I pointed it out.

"It's about Brett calling me dirty at the lunch table." I say, Emory's eyes falling to the ground.

It's about the term: "black-on-black crime" and the fact that there is no white equivalent to it.

It's about the man that easily called me a slur used to dehumanize and destroy my ancestors.

It's about the fact that the history books ignore all of black history. Black civilizations. Black empires. Black doctors, black scientists, black inventors, ancient black libraries and universities.

It's about the fact that black people get the shortest month of the year to celebrate our history and Elkwood can't even touch on it during then.

"It's about the drug jokes Brett's friends are always sending your way." Laura mutters, arms folded.

"It's about people who called me angry when I disagreed in English class." I say, more to myself than anyone else.

It's about so much more than one incident.

It's about the entire foundation of Elkwood. The curriculum, the lunch staff, the handbook, the monoethnic (and sometimes even unqualified) staff. It's about the very institutions of this state. Hell, this country.

Emory's eyes glaze over in thought, arms folded as everything wrong with the system comes crumbling down on us, revealing that Emory's incident is only a droplet in the swirling ocean of injustice that exists in Elkwood.

It barely scrapes the surface.

Laura meets each of our eyes, and Emory almost straightens in his seat as my group exchanges an electric look, centuries of unfairness coming to life in mere seconds.

It's that revelation that causes our invites to go all over social media, (courtesy of one Yasmine Abadi's insanely fast texting fingers.) It's that revelation that causes our pens and markers to run across posters faster and faster, bigger and brighter. Angrier and bolder. It's that revelation that causes us to make calls to other kids, kids we barely talk to. Anyone and everyone that'll listen. Telling them about what we're fighting for; why we're fighting for it.

It's that revelation that sets our revolution on fire.

protests at elkwood

My heart stutters.

Elkwood looms over me, all in its full glory, bricks standing firmly against the ground, a century old creation that resists to budge. At least, until someone makes it.

It's me alone down here, feet shifting on the sidewalk, hands gripping my poster. I'm trembling. The school stares back at me, unshaking.

My kilt is on, a few buttons of my shirt undone. Somewhere down the street, my parents are waiting in the car in order to provide extra backup. That is, until they have to leave. Until they have to drive over to work and catch the train downtown.

Nat is probably somewhere far behind, carefully watching everything unfold, eyes curious, stance wary.

Wind bristles my kilt. It seems like the air is sucked away from my lungs as I glance up at the building, cold biting at my exposed skin, everyone seeming worlds away.

Everything seems to melt away, like french vanilla ice cream on a hot summer's day. At least, as hot as it gets up here.

I need to take the first step. So, I do. I walk. My sign stays clenched between my fingers, soaking up the chilly air, just like I do. I'm making the first step, stepping into Elkwood territory. Everything can change.

I take another step, breathe a little, let the sun illuminate my skin as I enter the gates, up to the center area. Some kids are being dropped off— or dropping themselves off. Someone honks. And I should step back, you know? Let the day progress just like any other day at Elkwood. Let my resistance, my hurt and my pain fall away like discarded shards of glass.

I need to move. I need to speak. Because docility has never led to change. There's no choice other than raising my chin to the sun.

My hands clench around either side of my sign, and I raise that to the sun, too.

Some people stop. Hesitate. Squint out of their car windows to see what on earth is going on.

I raise my sign higher.

Chatter fills the front gates, the parking lot, the students loitering around the front of the school.

And then I cry out.

"*Where is my history?*" It's a yell of a question, and eyes dart to me, lips parting.

"What?" An elderly white lady calls out, glancing at me from the front of the school.

"Where is the black history in Elkwood?" I ask again, crying out, my sign reading what my voice is carrying. *Black history should matter to Elkwood.* Murmurs. A shorter man turns towards me, pushing glasses up his nose. A teacher.

I'm in the front space of the school, isolated as I push my sign into the air. My hair's free, forming curls that I'd never worn to school before today. I'd undid my braids over the weekend. And so, my tightly-wound curls fly to the sky and down to my shoulders, gleaming under the rays of sunlight.

"Excuse me, you're causing a disruption." It's the supervisor—Mrs. Mitchell. She pushes her glasses up her nose. "Head to class."

Class for who? I should ask.

Regardless, class starts in fifteen minutes, I've made sure of that. My sign, however, will stay up for the whole day. It *has* to.

I don't respond, don't lower my sign. My heart stumbles along with my breathing. All I'm hoping is that my stance doesn't reveal that. I can't shake, I can't falter.

Mrs. Mitchell glances around. There's nervousness for sure. Because the students are watching me, scattered about. A few parents peer out of the windows of their car. And, *God*, it's the scariest thing. It feels like my legs will give way and I'll just fall to the ground.

But, they don't.

Mrs. Mitchell reaches for me, and I swerve out of her grasp, my sign still held high.

"Hand the sign over. This isn't the time nor the place." She says, grasping for me again, grasping for the sign that illustrates the truth that she doesn't want anyone to see.

I stumble backwards, just barely catching my step, and Mrs. Mitchell shakes a head of dyed blonde hair. "You're going to hand that sign over or head over to Ms. Anderson. Stop stirring up trouble."

I suck in a breath, almost cornered as Mrs. Mitchell adjusts the bright orange vest, eyes narrowing.

Breaths come in and out, again and again and again.

We're almost at an impasse.

If she takes the sign, she'll rip it up, send me to the office. Then, everything will be over.

Brett will go about his life with his troop. They'll continue breaking rules, attacking students, letting smugly racist comments slip from their lips.

I'll go back to sitting at the corner of the class, feet pointed inwards, head down as black history— *my* history goes ignored.

And our makeshift group? Likely to go in all different directions. Emory might move away. Just a week ago, he said that his parents might consider it. And after sending emails to the school about the whole incident—emails that went *unanswered*—why wouldn't they? Their son might not be safe here. It's one of the best schools in the district, but if nothing is going to change, if Brett walks away without repercussions, then what's left for them here?

Laura might stay at my table. Most likely she will. We'll exchange sardonic grins, talk about everything wrong with that day's history class. With the alliance done, Yasmine might return to her old table. We might trade nods or maybe even wave as we pass each other in the hallway.

Then that'll be it. I'll graduate with the highest grades, but Olivia will be valedictorian, just because. And if they *do* ask me to speak, I'll grin, tell them about how this school pushed me to my limits, helped me form strong bonds, *yada yada yada.*

My heart shatters at the thought.

And something in me is ignited. Something in Mrs. Mitchell's eyes sees it too.

I open my mouth, ready to cry out my pain, cry out the truth.

But then, there's a roar.

It's not like any roar I've ever heard, either. Not just the call of a beast—the call of a cry. A call of pain.

"Decolonize the curriculum." And it's Laura. She's taking firm steps, chin pointed towards the skies, skin reflecting the brightest sun. The sign hangs up in the air. "Where's our precolonial history?" She cries out, glancing about the space, twin braids swinging with her.

Mrs. Mitchell steps back.

"I belong here." It's Yasmine, pants flowing, eyes strong, blazer hanging from her torso. "There's no place for hate in Elkwood!"

"My burns are on Elkwood's hands." And, God, it's Emory. And he's resisting. For the first time since I've ever met him, he's letting his *hurt* show.

Then they're beside me, signs in the air, the four of us aligned, the rest of Elkwood facing us.

Mrs. Mitchell gathers herself together, raising a finger as she opens her mouth to say something.

Then I hear footsteps, and it isn't just tiny pitter patters. No, it's a slight thunder. It's when I turn around—glancing behind me— that I see them.

Elkwood.

Not the Elkwood that's seated in their cars, eyes suspiciously analyzing the scene. Not the Elkwood that's nudging each other, jeering at the four of us. Not the Elkwood that's shaking their heads, averting their eyes from everything. Because they won't see what they don't want to see.

Even though pretending won't make it disappear.

But the Elkwood that *I* see is surging behind us, a steady current of students. I see Millie, braces on, eyes intense as she pushes her sign into the air. Then there's Walt— the absurdly unapologetic Walt— and he's chanting next to them, glasses reflecting the sunlight.

I hear a deep, booming, "People didn't die so that we could erase them!" A tall senior, hair tousled in all directions.

"Stop censoring history class!" It's Jennifer, black strands of hair falling to her hips, her sign pushed into the faces of the administration. Mia wheels down the courtyard of the school. "Tell us our full history! Tell us our Black and Indigenous history."

Then an Ambiguous White makes her way next to her. She calls something out, sunglasses on as she pushes her sign into the air. "Every student should matter to Elkwood!" Then another yell. "Hold Elkwood accountable!"

The world is spinning.

My world is spinning.

Because, for the first time in a millennia, I see people around me, behind me, with me. Their chants call for a decolonization of the school's curriculum, to properly address the evils performed by some of our nation's founders, to call for attention to the burns on Emory William's body.

To pressure the administration.

I can feel my hands shaking slightly, posture still firm, stance still wide. My eyes flit about the space, and it's all I can do to remind myself to *breathe*.

As our chants and calls rise to the blue sky, I feel limitless. Laura sends a smile my way, one of her tilted little lip quirks, the one that is hard not to return, the *we got this* grin.

Our calls are our war song. A song that's been playing on repeat for the past five hundred years, hidden deep in our hearts but unwilling to slip out.

I think of my ancestors who wove maps into cornrows, maps to freedom. I think of the songs with hidden stories, hidden maps; the way to liberation. I think of black cowboys, the ranches they settled, the cultures they created. I think of the black kingdoms I never learned about during history class. I think of my namesake.

I think of everything.

And from the ground, I can hear the sorrowful melody of my ancestors, rising through the cracks of the concrete. That painful melody infuses me with so *much* that my body quivers with everything.

I'm powerful.

We are.

A sharp voice cuts through the air, startling me out of my thoughts. The students around and behind me slow their cries, glancing at each other.

The school doors open, a low creaking sound piercing through the air. It's followed by sharp *clacks* down the front steps. My eyes drift up to a black suit, a skirt that firmly stops at the knees, and a suit jacket paired with a pearl necklace.

Glasses frame her eyes, and there's almost a collective sucking of air as Ms. Anderson clicks down the main entrance, glancing about the space, meeting each student's face with a stern glance.

"What's going on?" She asks, and the mood seems to shift. People glance around, murmuring slightly. Eyes find Ms. Anderson's shiny heels.

"Well?" She asks, letting out a little scoff, eyes tracing the space. "Anyone care to tell me who's in charge, then?"

Wind answers her.

Her stoic bun stays composed, lipstick redder than anything within a five-mile parameter. "Alrighty," she scans the space, eyes finally landing on me.

"Amina Davis, please meet me in the office." She says, eyes zeroing in on me.

I suck in a breath. Murmurs of disquiet fill the air. At this, Ms. Anderson smoothes down her dark skirt and walks back into the school, but not before saying, "the rest of you should be heading to your classes. The bell rings in less than five minutes."

A self-satisfied grin curls onto Mrs. Mitchell's lips as she urges the students back inside the building, many of them glancing back at me. I feel a few gentle nudges, some shoulder pats. Yasmine and Emory hover about before being swept into the crowd of students, sending concerned glances my way.

Laura stays.

"Want me to come with you?" She asks, lips pursed as she slides her sign underneath her arm.

"You'd get into trouble," I say, letting my shoulders fall. "She asked for me."

"Guess so," Laura says, lips pursed. "But kind of rough for me to send you into the lion's den alone, isn't it? You were doing this for *my* campaign. We're equally responsible."

"I came up with the idea, remember?" I say, one of those sorrowful, lopsided grins curling onto my lips as I make my way up the front steps, Laura in step with me.

"So, what?" She asks, blinking underneath the bright lighting.

"*So*, I'm not about to let you get in trouble. Besides, Ms. Anderson already has her eye on you, don't want to stoke the flame."

We're inside the school building by now. I hold my books to my chest, glancing around the space, eyes falling to the clear office where Ms. Anderson resides.

"Not too sure how I feel about this." Laura says, holding onto the straps of her backpack as it swings from side to side.

"Me neither," I reply honestly, tilting my head to the side, curls tickling at my neck. "But you're really gonna be late if you stay back here."

Laura lets out a breath.

I shoo her away, smile a little, give her a lazy salute once her shoulders fall in acquiescence. Then she's down the hall, a teacher beckoning her into the classroom. She sends a glance my way. Then she's gone.

With that, I turn on my heel, taking a painful gulp as I edge closer to the office, breaths speeding once my eyes catch onto a grey door that reads: *Rebecca Anderson.*

The secretary stares at me from behind her clear desk, eyeing me from where she's seated, fingers halted and hovering over her black computer.

She then gives the subtlest of nods, a jut of the head towards Anderson's Notorious Grey Door™. It's one that I've been lucky enough to avoid for most of my time here.

At least, up until recently. Because now, I'm stepping into that notorious room, and I have a million future possibilities for what can occur. None of them are good.

I knock. Silence greets me as I push the door further open. Ms. Anderson is seated at her desk, glasses slipping down the slope of her nose, everything about the room being just as tedious as it's known for.

The clock ticks. Ms. Anderson glances up at me, gesturing towards the chair. The fact that she hasn't said anything since I've stepped into the room is frighteningly eerie, and I'm not the least bit fond of the fact.

Painful minutes drag by.

I inhale, exhale. Somehow, my breaths feel unsteady. I have to wonder whether or not Ms. Anderson enjoys this, watching bits of my sanity drip away as she slowly drives me insane.

She's always striked me as a sadist.

"Miss Davis," Her tone comes out in clips.

I meet her eyes.

"What on earth was this, today?" She asks. Her voice is saccharine, but with an edge. Almost like a kindergarten teacher talking to a silly little kid that made a mess on the carpet floor.

I swallow, look up. "A statement?"

Ms. Anderson laughs. "I think the word you're looking for is *disruption*."

The clock keeps ticking.

I say nothing. Nothing because if I correct her, Anderson's cloying facade will fall to dust.

"It's so unlike you." She shakes her head. "You're normally such a staid girl." A chuckle, cold eyes freezing mine. "It's one reason you've been able to stay in this school."

She leans forward, slowly shaking her head. "You are *very* lucky to be here."

I've heard it once, I've heard it twice. I've heard it all my life.

You're lucky to be here. As though I haven't put my everything into being here. As though I'm an outsider that *just* managed to slide her way into this place. As if my existence is barely condoned, barely tolerated.

"And causing disruptions like this?" She asks, "I have to say, I'm disappointed. It'll force me to take action." She purses her lips tightly. "Your actions do not represent the values of a strong student, especially not here at Elkwood."

I swallow, cool the rising flames of my mind. "With all due respect, Ms. Anderson," I say, "I think my statement *does* represent values of a strong student."

There's something resembling a scoff that slips from her lips. "In what way, exactly?"

"Uh," I breathe. "I'm trying to communicate with the administration of Elkwood in the best way I know how, especially given the fact that I initially tried to convey my thoughts to you the other day, but—"

"*But* you showed me grainy footage of an alleged incident with no context." Ms. Anderson cuts in, eyes staring me down.

"I showed you a clip of a student confessing to several offenses against our code of conduct. I don't think there's much else I can supply to clarify the situation."

"As I stated before, I'll need to have a word with said student before I can take any action." She says, chin resting on her hands.

"But what does that mean for Emory?" I ask, leaning forward in my chair. "*Someone* attacked him."

"You don't take things into your own hands, Amina. That's what authority does. It's not your prerogative." Ms. Anderson says, my words falling to deaf ears.

My mind feels like an ocean of: *I just can't think.* Because despite the evidence, Ms. Anderson refuses to directly address what happened. If she does end up having the conversation with Brett, he'll sweet talk his way out of it. She'll let him go.

She always does.

My heart clenches. *The footage isn't enough.* None of it would ever be enough. We're losing.

"And I'm afraid that your discrepancies warrant consequences."

My head is throbbing.

"There is no doubt that something happened to Emory Richards, but I will be sure to address that on a later date. Your involvement is only going to be detrimental for *your* future here at Elkwood."

The world is crashing.

My breaths come in and out, chest heaves up and down, and I can't stop them. I'm physically incapable.

But the door of the office opens, startling me out of my lucid nightmare.

Both Ms. Anderson and I whip around to the doorway. And standing at the center of it is Tyler Thompson.

At this point, I don't think all is lost anymore.

I *know* it.

Not to mention that his parents are flanking either side of him. The last thing I need right now is any of Brett's posse getting involved in this. It can't mean anything good for me.

His parents look expectant, his dad's eyes furrowed, his mom's hair in light waves. They're looking down at their son who offers me a brief glance before trilling his lips awkwardly.

It's clear that the Thompsons have something to say.

"Oh, Mr and Mrs. Thompson," Ms. Anderson grins, rising to her feet, voice honey and sweet, everything about her tone utterly different than it was just seconds ago. "Tyler." She gives him a nod. "What a pleasant surprise." A pause. "Hopefully, the short-lived craziness out here hasn't been too much of a concern to you." She weaves around her desk. "I can assure you that discipline will be inflicted on all those involved."

Thompson's dad grunts, his mom offers a polite smile.

"Is there anything I can do to help you all today?"

“Tyler has something to share, if that’s alright with you.” Mr. Thompson grunts again, and I briefly wonder if that’s his primary form of communication.

Mrs. Thompson nudges him forward, lips pulled into a too-tight grin. Tyler lets out a light groan, shuffles forward. He glances at me again, glances at his parents, glances at Ms. Anderson.

Redness dusts his face, and it’s somewhat concerning to see Tyler Thompson looking anxious. I can’t tell whether or not that’s a good thing or a bad thing.

“I, uh,” he runs a hand through his hair, “have a video.”

He slips his phone out of his back pocket, glancing warily at his parents.

Ms. Anderson knits her eyebrows together, making her way closer to the screen, eyes squinted.

The video starts. There are some yells, rowdy laughter. Immediately, I can trace the signature barks of laughter back to the White Bros™.

In the video, the ground is dirt, trunks of evergreens everywhere in sight. The video's vertical, camera positioned towards the ground, changing angles every few seconds, shaking constantly.

The mood shifts when a '*what the hell are you doing?*' breaks from one voice. Emory's voice.

There's a crunch of underbrush underfoot.

"Wait, I just want to see something."

A laugh. Speeding footsteps.

The click of a lighter.

"*Wait, hold still.*"

"*Get the hell away from me.*"

"*We're just messing around, calm down.*"

The video shifts to Emory's face. He's backed against a tree trunk, arms outstretched like he's ready to throw a few punches but knows he shouldn't.

"*Whoops.*"

Fire on skin.

A yell.

And again, and again, and again.

The laughter is in the background, teasing and malicious and everything *wrong.*

From behind the camera, "*guys, I think we should stop.*"

There's a grunt and a dry laugh, no one paying any heed to the voice of caution. Then there's another yell. Sizzling. Fire on skin. *More fire on skin.* Brett's leading most of the attacks, but others join in. Swears light up the background.

I feel nauseous.

A push. Another swear.

Emory limps away.

"*You think we went too far?*"

"*Shut up, Tyler.*"

The video goes black.

The room is silent.

Mrs. Thompson holds a hand over her mouth, eyes welling up. Tyler's gaze falls to the ground. His dad glances away, lips pursed.

Ms. Anderson's lips are parted.

Finally, Mrs. Thompson seems to find words. "We found this video on Tyler's phone, and were shocked to see something so awful on it."

"We believe it'd be very wrong," Mr. Thompson adds, "for us to keep it in the dark. So, we brought it to your attention as soon as we found out."

"You don't know how disappointed we are." Mrs. Thompson says. Tyler keeps his gaze on the floor. "But this should be addressed as soon as possible. And Tyler will also be apologizing to Emory. But we also realize that this violates the Elkwood Code of Conduct, so Tyler is ready to accept the consequences as you see fit."

Ms. Anderson doesn't glance back in my direction. She rubs her temples, lets out a breath. But with this blatant evidence, I can't see any way for her to work around it.

An incident like this could mean juvenile detention. It's crossed the line of bullying and dangerously ventured into the realm of assault. And everyone in this room is fully aware of the fact.

The video seems infinitely worse than anything Emory described. The sizzling of fire against skin reverberates in my mind nothing short of a million times.

"Thank you for bringing this to my attention," Ms. Anderson says, composure barely held together. She squints as though still attempting to process the video.

She walks back to her desk slowly and vacantly. Almost as though she's half-awake, half-aware.

She swallows, eyes glazed over. Then, she holds down the button of the mic. "Brett McGill, please report to the front office."

So, that's what it is. McGill.

"Mr and Mrs. Thompson," Ms. Anderson starts as though it physically pains her to say it, "please remain here."

I suck in a breath, my mind still trying to process what just happened.

"You may leave, Miss Davis," Ms. Anderson says vacantly, eyes still blank and lost.

She doesn't have to tell me twice.

election day

Brett getting suspended is the single most shocking thing that's occurred this year.

And given that this year has been absolute *chaos*, that's saying something.

All curled up in the school library, I sink into the bright orange bean bag that's almost scathing to the eyes. After a few seconds, an incredulous gust of air escapes my lips.

He really got suspended. Brett is the type of person to command all attention within a four-mile radius, to be heard over the most rampant storm. So, his absence is potent the day after he gets suspended, alongside a quarter of the school's lacrosse team.

Tucking a curl behind my ear, I inhale the atmosphere, almost trying to soak up as much peace as I can.

Interestingly enough, Tyler Thompson got off with a three-day-suspension and some cafeteria work. I'm guessing it's due to his lack of direct involvement in the whole thing.

Trilling my lips, I tilt my head to the side. But *still*, he was there, and he did *nothing* to stop them.

Brett and the rest of the team didn't get it as easy as Thomspon. What *they* got was a solid week of suspension.

Ms. Anderson had called a short assembly, vaguely stating that violence of any kind wasn't tolerated at Elkwood and didn't respect our values.

She never actually explained the incident.

But honestly, it doesn't matter, because the incident and the suspensions that it resulted in have been spreading like wildfire.

I purse my lips, eyes flicking up to the ceiling.

I wasn't even the first to know. After having gone back to class, Laura had grilled me about the events that took place in Ms. Anderson's room, and I'd finally filled her in during lunch.

The next evening, I'd been propped onto my bed when I received all-caps text messages from one Yasmine Abadi. They went something like: *Did you hear? Brett got suspended. He got suspended. This is crazy, I-*

Moreover, Yasmine's frantic messages summed up everything that had taken place. Emory had texted to say that the school would be paying for his treatment, the burns that were gradually getting better, and Laura had sent me recordings primarily featuring her hysterical laughter.

"Amina!"

With the sound of my name, my eyes dart around the library. Mahogany, books that smell like leaves and musk, the *tap tap tap* of the librarian typing on her laptop. And finally, my eyes settle on Laura Johnson.

"Laura," I call out, returning her grin solely because her grins are contagious like that.

She flops down next to me, the beanbag sinking as she glances over at me.

"You don't know how satisfying it is to see Brett—God *forbid*—held accountable," she grabs hold of my shoulders, silver and fabric bracelets clinking as she does so, "the whole thing was *surreal*, Amina."

I shake my head, smile still unfailing, "honestly."

"If you ask me," Laura starts, lips pursed as she gives me a brief glance, "he should've gotten expelled." A shrug. "Personally, I'd take it to court."

A laugh slides from my lips. "You definitely would."

"What can I say?" She asks, lips quirking upwards as her dark hair presses against the plush. "I don't know when to stop fighting."

She exhales a melodic chuckle, flicking at my forehead. "You know that."

Rubbing my forehead, I roll my eyes somewhat teasingly. "Don't I know it."

"It's served me," she says, nodding solemnly, eyes taking over a vacant expression. "Did it serve me *well?* That's the question."

“Top ten unsolved mysteries,” I mutter, as Laura chuckles again, the sound slightly raspy and yet sprinkled with genuine amusement.

“Something like that,” she says, one of her feet nudging against mine as the other taps on the carpeted flooring.

“All dressed up for election day, I see,” I say, Laura’s eyes brightening.

“I should give you, like, a mini fashion show,” she says, rising to her feet as she adjusts the gray blazer necessary for her speech today, dark combat boots tapping against the ground.

Her dark combat boots are most likely going to irritate some teachers. Because despite the fact that it technically *doesn’t* commit any transgressions against the oh-so-mighty dress code, it is narrowly tolerated.

It might look too ‘punk’ to them, or ‘trashy’. I can’t be certain what vocabulary they’re likely to use in this case. But seeing as Laura has never been one to utterly co-exist with order, it won’t have much of an effect, anyway.

Meanwhile, the rest of her outfit consists of the dark kilt, pale dress shirt and gray and red tie, hair cascading down her shoulders as she practices a politician-esque smile at me as she gives a twirl.

"This is perfect," I let out a chuckle as Laura laughs, sliding into the seat she was in before.

"Kind of anxious," she says, lips pursed, "but, we'll see how things turn out."

"Just remember to breathe," I say, her hand outstretched, ready to shake mine as though we're two business partners who have completed a major deal. Our hands meet like two old friends, and Laura nods in response.

Her lips quirk upwards into something teasing. "Keep the oxygen coming in. Got it."

***

As we all usher towards the auditorium, I'm pressed against the sides of bustling students, eyebrows flying upwards once I feel a tap on my shoulder.

Sure enough, it's Yasmine, Emory not too far behind as they fall into step with me.

"How're your burns?" I ask, Emory glancing down at me with a half-grin.

"Doing alright," he says, grin still only halfway there.

"And your parents?" Yasmine asks from my other side, the three of us brushing against each other as we make our way down the hall. Emory trills his lips, runs a hand through dark curls.

"Could be better," he finally says as we turn a corner. "They're still a bit shaken up about the whole thing. They're not too sure about keeping me in school when Brett's going to return."

His words puncture the air.

"Are you moving?" Yasmine asks, voice softening.

"I honestly don't know," Emory runs a hand through his curls once more. "Like, you can't just pack up your stuff and leave. My parents were born and raised here, and so was I." An easy shrug. "Plus, moving means another job in another state. But you know, maybe that's the better option." He rolls his shoulders back, eyebrows knitting together. "That being said, it honestly feels kind of gross to be run out of the town by racists. Like they've won or something."

He glances between the two of us, eyes searching our faces. "As of now, there are a lot of emails being sent, and safety precautions being instilled in my mind. *Incessantly.* Personally, I think they're a bit over the top, but..." he trails off.

"It's safer," I say quietly, almost as though reminding myself.

"Yeah," his eyes catch onto mine before he continues, "and I mean, I don't have anything as serious as third degree burns or anything." *Extreme second degree burns are still damaging,* I think, but choose not to say.

Emory plows on, "I'm pretty sure that my mom thinks I have some major trauma from the whole thing."

"Do you?" Yasmine asks, dark eyes inquisitive as we make our way through open doors, Emory slapping the top of the doorway on our way through.

"Listen, I don't know." He exhales. "All I know is I'd like the last of *these,*" he gestures over slight bruises on his chin and covered arms, "to be gone."

"Understandable," I say, as we pull into the auditorium, finding seats towards the center. We plop down onto the velvet seats, our eyes finding the stage where a lone podium stands.

"And yeah," he says, lips pursing as he analyzes the outside of his hand. "Skin grafting isn't all that fun. Luckily, everything else just needed antibiotic cream."

There's a silence, then Yasmine runs an exhausted hand over her forehead. "What they did was disgusting. I'm sorry."

"Well, Brett had to drop out of the race. That has to count for something," Emory says, shrugging easily.

Before anything else can be said, the assembly kicks off and Ms. Anderson makes her way to the podium, clasping her hands together as the auditorium quiets.

Her introduction is neutral, tone calm as she lists the candidates. What started out as four has shrunk down to two. From the front row, Laura purses her lips, turning back and shooting a grin once she finds us.

The introduction comes to a brisk end, people murmuring as Walt makes his way onto the stage, blazer and dress pants gleaming underneath the bright lights.

And then he starts. It's simple words, calm words. He seems more put-together than I've ever seen him, a fact that is remarkable given that most people in the auditorium are more stressed than I've ever seen them.

He glances up, eyes flicking from person to person behind the thick lenses of his glasses. He makes light promises, thinks out loud, exhales some gentle attempts at humor, closes with an easy nod that almost contradicts his feet tapping incessantly on the stage floor.

And with an easy transition, Laura steps forward, eyes firm and expression serene.

Of course, she does amazingly. She speaks like a river, a steady flow of a current. She has nothing to prove, and she knows it. She only lightly touches on the suspension note, opening herself up as she briefly touches on her story. People exchange glances, almost as though trying to weigh whether or not it matters at this point.

After all, Brett's been suspended, too.

Not that it matters, though. Especially seeing as there are only two options, and the student body has to lean to either Walter Cohen or Laura Johnson. And both candidates are attempting to cross the gaping bridge separating themselves from the rest of the student body.

Who's crossed the bridge? We'll know soon enough.

Once Laura wraps up her speech, she strolls offstage, settling down in the seat next to Walter, both of whom shake each other's hands before their gazes return to the front.

With that, the ballots are sent to us, the pinging of the notifications showing up on school-designated devices. And with that, we take note of both options on the ballot.

WALTER COHEN.

LAURA JOHNSON.

There's a write-in option on the ballot, but my eyes skip over it. Without much thought, I click the check next to Laura's name, mentally sending good vibes to Walter as I do so. Setting my phone aside, I glance about the room. Some people don't even have their devices out, Leslie and Amber standing out within the midst of the throng.

Amber dropped out too early in the race. By the time that Brett was forced to drop out, it was too late for her to restart her campaign. Deadlines had passed, people had moved on. Something that she's obviously still irritated about.

Leslie had wanted us to beat Brett on Amber's behalf. And now that we've somehow done that—or more so, Brett did that himself (with the help of the Thompsons, of course)—there's no reason for her to care about the race.

Despite myself, a dry laugh escapes my lips. Not surprising in the least bit.

I glance over at Emory and Yasmine, who've wasted no time filling out the ballots and submitting them. All I'm hoping is that enough people care enough to vote.

The voting process has always been short in the school. After all, some people have already voted, given that the window opened yesterday. That being said, there are a solid number of teachers in the IT room, making sure nothing sketchy went on.

Once the votes are collected, the option to vote is locked. And now, we wait. Leaving the auditorium, our classes bleed by. The day inches by, and Laura is uncharacteristically quiet throughout, the only sign of emotion being her tapping feet on the marble flooring.

And finally, *finally*, the assembly arrives. The one that has wrought chaos and suspensions and stress. Anxiety, too. But now is the time that our apprehension gets lifted, either to give way to neutrality or slight relief.

Or disappointment.

But given that people have essentially *guessed* which candidate to pick—in the same way most of them utilise the faultless strategy of *eeny meeny miny moe* on their multiple choice tests— this election could truly go to either person.

All I'm hoping is that I did something right in managing. Otherwise all the heightened stress might not be worth it. The effort, the emails, and the posters might not be worth it.

But, I shake the thoughts from my mind as quickly as they arrive. What we've done here—president or not— has caused more than a ripple. Our success shouldn't hang on Laura's win.

That being said, I know Laura has a multitude of ideas. I know she's invested. I know she's nervous, given her silence throughout the entire day.

While I don't know what the election results will bring, I know one thing for sure. I exhale a dry laugh as I make my way into the auditorium with the flurry of students, making a solid promise to myself.

I am never going into politics again.

Soon enough, I'm in the auditorium, all the expectant faces pointed towards the stage as Ms. Anderson makes her way back to the podium, an envelope in hand.

"And, your new Stu-Co member is..." She opens the envelope, slips the paper out of it. Her eyes squint as she takes in the sheet.

Trying to gauge the expressions of the students, I mentally will them to remember everything. To remember the way Laura inspired them that way in the cafeteria. The way she reached out to them, talked *to* them instead of *at* them,

I hope they remember.

I hope they remember the way I crawled out of the shadows and put my life into this campaign, because somewhere deep inside of me, I wanted a change.

I wanted *Elkwood* to change. And I wanted to be the one who orchestrated that change.

Ms. Anderson raises the paper to her face, eyes scanning over it.

Her lips move.

The auditorium sucks in a collective breath.

"Walter Cohen."

Walter blinks from his seat in the front, Ms. Anderson squints once more. My chest squeezes, both tentatively supportive of Walter but devastated that Laura hasn't won.

Ms. Anderson's lips move as she continues, "as your vice president, second in command."

The world seems deafening in that moment as my mind tries to process what that means. Applause rises around me, but all I seem to hear is the atmosphere screaming and euphoria threatening to seep from my chest.

Laura doesn't move, doesn't even blink.

Ms. Anderson pauses. "Making Laura Johnson Stu-Co president."

The auditorium rumbles in confusion, people shouting, eyes flicking to each person.

Ms. Anderson hushes the crowd.

She plows on. "The two were also very close in votes."

Ms. Anderson just shakes her head as the auditorium quiets. "This year, your student council will hopefully look more like a co-presidency," she says, her voice thin. "This is a very unique year in Elkwood history. But given the situation, the administration has decided to try something new." An exhaled breath. "Would Walter Cohen and Laura Johnson please join me onstage?"

There are slight murmurs as they rise to their feet, applause rumbling in the air.

The two make their way onstage, expressions semi-amused if not slightly bemused as Ms. Anderson brings them to the front and shakes their hands.

Walt seems nearly breathless, Ms. Anderson passive as Laura reaches over to shake his hands. There's a smile in her eyes that is reflected by him, and I start to think that maybe this Stu-Co presidency will be something new. Something better.

And with the crowd erupting around me, my world seems just a bit brighter. Somehow, Laura's eyes find me from where she stands onstage.

There's a nod, and then she sends me a grin that shatters universes. In return, I send her one that elicits supernovas.

little changes

Winning is a strange feeling.

It feels foreign. This feeling of absolute euphoria that's unlike anything I've ever felt before.

We won.

Laura Johnson is Elkwood's president. The outspoken, unapologetically Sioux, Laura Johnson is Stu-Co president alongside Walter Cohen who is ready to redefine the very concept of Elkwood's vice-presidency, morph it into a power that might be so much *more.*

When I'd arrived home that day, Mom and Dad seemed to see the pure euphoria pooling out of my chest, because Mom had grabbed my shoulders, shooting me a million questions a minute.

"How did Ms. Anderson take the protest? Are you okay? Is Laura okay? How are Emory's burns? How did the elections go?"

And I'd spilled everything out. Delirious laughs escaped my lips as I told them everything. Told them about nearly getting in trouble before the Thompsons showed up. Told them about the suspensions. Told them about Laura's win and all the details surrounding it.

Told them everything.

As of now, I'm back at school with Laura, her shoes clicking against the marble as she fills me in on all her propositions. Some additions to the history curriculum featuring pre-colonial civilizations. Featuring the Americas before October 12, 1492. Featuring aspects of her history gone untold.

My history included. History featuring Frederick Douglass, the pre-colonial history of my own ancestors. The kingdoms, the empires. But it doesn't stop there, because Laura's already delved into different sects of our school, spoke to different people, jotted down ideas. Walter has brought his own ideas to the table as well, both sharing their notes, talking to different groups.

"We're also talking to the administration about the photo you mentioned," Laura says, tugging me out of my thoughts as I glance over at her, supplies held to my chest.

"Yeah?" I ask, falling into step with her as I urge her to continue talking.

"Yeah," she nods with one of those grins as we turn a corner, "we're hoping that they'll give Elkwood's non-white people more of a voice." She purses her lips, eyes meeting mine. "Rather than just being used for good publicity."

"I like the sound of that," I say softly, Laura's grin widening.

"So do I," she says, her eyes flickering away from my face and to something ahead of us. "And there's Walter right now." She turns to me with a wink. "We'll be going over points together. For lunch."

"Alright," I say, my fingers wiggling in a slight wave. Laura makes a move to leave before retracing her steps. My eyebrows fly upwards as her arm swings over my shoulder and her expression morphs into something almost relieved.

"Thank you," she says, eyes serene. "Thank you for campaigning with me." A pause as her eyes crinkle. "We made it, Amina." She repeats it slowly. "We really made it."

"For sure," I say as she pulls away. A teasing grin flickers to my lips. "Now it's time to actually get things done." I give her a nudge. "Don't disappoint."

"You know me," She says, that lightning grin back. "I never disappoint." And with that, her eyes flicker and she's down the hall, Walt slowing down as she falls into step with him, both delving into conversation.

Somehow, seeing their frames retreat down the hall, there's a feeling of *right* that permeates through the walls of Elkwood. From the absence of racist taunts in the hallway to the tentative grins exchanged between different students.

It's not perfect, of course.

The students that would've loyally voted for either Amber or Brett still send those cold looks as I pass them in the hallway. Jokes about the write-in votes still fly from locker to locker. Whenever I pass either Leslie, Amber, or Ms. Anderson in the hallway, not one of them sends a glance my way.

Letting out a laugh, I curve into the debate room, Mr. Pham glancing up from his desk and sending me a bright grin.

I return it.

And while imperfections might be prominent. The stars almost seem to be aligning.

***

The scent of pure *library* rises to the atmosphere as Ms. Knox grins at me from the front desk.

"Amina?" she asks, tilting her head to the side. A summer grin breaks out onto her lips. "Long time no see."

"Seriously," I exhale a breath as her hazel eyes find mine. "It feels like forever since I've been here." My eyes flicker about the space as the memory comes to me. "When I, uh broke down."

"Happens to the best of us," Ms. Knox says, arms resting on her desk as a blue ballpoint pen is embedded in her curls. I'm about to let her know about said pen, but instead I settle with a silent laugh.

"I guess." I say, head tilted to the side as a faint grin rises to my lips.

"And it's okay," Ms. Knox assures me, rising to her feet as she adjusts the waistband of her wide jeans, the floral top that she wears over her torso. "You seem happier. At least, you seem content. Like you're doing okay."

My thumb traces over my bottom lip in thought. "I'm smiling more, I think."

"So," Ms. Knox starts, weaving around her desk as she tosses an arm over my shoulder. "How's life been treating you?"

"It's been a *trip,*" I reply, adjusting the elastic that contains my curly bun. Curls spill out, and I tuck one behind my ear as I shake my head, the past few months crashing down on me like a ton of bricks.

Ms. Knox hums, a grin appearing on her lips. "Tell you what," she glances down at me, huge glasses slipping down the bridge of her nose. "You're going to fill me in on it." A sparkling grin as she offers a suggestion. "Café?"

I return the grin, and Ms. Knox swoops her bag over the shoulder as I nod. "Café."

***

A couple of weeks later, the photo ends up being taken. This time, however, it consists of volunteers, people who genuinely want to be part of the photo. And this time, it's a natural setting. People seated around the table and delving into their lunches as they talk and laugh.

And I'm there, seated right next to Yasmine Abadi as she tells me something about her vacation and infinite stories that slip from her lips without much thought.

Being around so many other students used to be hellish. Elkwood was an ocean of lights, but I was the only one drowning.

However, now? With Yasmine's arm slung around me, bringing me close, the henna curving up her hands visible underneath the sunlight.

She's laughing, dark bun bobbing as she shakes her head. There's the sound of a shutter, a brief flash. Emory's across from us, seated next to Walter, a plethora of get-well cards and apology letters held in a bright bag seated on his lap. His burns are fading, his smile a bit wider.

He might move. The option is still up in the air, his parents mulling over whether or not to press charges. Charges mean a legal battle, and that means money and time and effort. As of now, though, he seems almost carefree, the effortless beauty of him captured by every camera flash.

Of course, Yasmine is smiling like summer, Jennifer Zhang behind the camera, light jokes filling the air like the universe belongs to us. Always has.

And so, I allow myself to feel *okay*. Just this once. As okay as my performance in the debate, one that has plunged me toward a spot at nationals. As okay as Yasmine's autumn voice and the weather that's less frigid than it was months ago.

As okay as the smile painting my lips in rainbow. And the panic attacks that have been subsiding. There, but not nearly as frequent. Unlikely to disappear, but no longer dominating every aspect of my life.

And for once, *for once* I genuinely feel okay.

the cookout

Mr. Johnson is grand.

He's one of those grandiose people, standing at a solid 6'2". Silent like the night, and the epitome of the calm that comes after the storm.

His hair is growing back. Wispy strands of night, just long enough for them to hover over his chin. He seems happy in the midst of the festivities and sunlight that dominate the area.

Stalks of fresh grass make up the space, the summer sun beating down on the ground, grass strands attempting to reach out and catch a few beams of light.

We seem to live in the sun.

My parents are here, only a little ways away, my uncle by the grill, his wife flipping the sizzling pieces of meat.

Mr. Johnson doesn't normally say a ton, but when he does, his voice carries through the atmosphere, and Laura smiles like her dad is everything and more than all the oceans combined.

My hands slip into my pockets as my eyes flicker over the space. My pale white shirt is tucked into paint-splattered jeans, everything about the braids that make their way down to my elbows screaming *sun.*

Emory Richards is here. His burns are gone. The day Brett had returned to school premises, he didn't say much. Of course, there were still the occasional comments, the lacrosse team trying to recapture what it was they had before.

Despite their efforts, however, I don't think it's possible for them to recreate it. And they had seemed to think so, too, because the group had broken off into smaller subgroups. I'm certain some of their parents had issued orders of avoidance; ones that had (halfheartedly) been carried out.

There's a faint flush to Emory's features, healthy and blooming beneath the sun.

He's laughing.

Off to the side is his older sister, hair a mess of almond curls, eyes bright as her floral dress billows in the wind. Look a little further back and you'll see his parents, deep into conversation with Laura's.

Once my eyes catch onto Emory Richards, his lips turn into a lopsided grin. He doesn't glance away. This time, he raises his can of soda to the atmosphere, and I mime clinking my glass with his.

Orion is here, organizing a little game of soccer with Claudie and her friends, the little kids glancing up at him, one dribbling the ball from foot to foot. Nat is next to him, arm slung around the former's shoulders.

And like his namesake, Orion's eyes seem to reflect the galaxy. His lips are pulled into a neutral line, but his eyes seem to glow.

Of course Ms. Knox is here. She's seated at one of the outdoor tables, knife and fork oh-so-gracefully cutting into the burger seated in front of her. Yasmine is speaking excitedly to her, Ms. Knox most likely dishing out book recs.

My eyes flicker over to Laura once more. Even during a day as light as this, Laura's shirt is a deep read, reading *MMIW.* She's thrown campaigns over the past few months before school closed for summer. Awareness posters have been hung in the hallways, always present.

An arm is slung around my shoulder, startling me out of my thoughts. It's so familiar that the aura has grown on me. A scent of autumn and sweetness and the cold atmosphere that's given way to the warmth of summer.

"Laura," I say, a grin sliding onto my lips as I look out onto the barbecue sight, filled from corner to corner with my family. Chosen and biological.

"Amina," she echoes in the same tone, black ponytail swishing from side to side.

"I'm happy you're here." I say, Laura grinning over at me like we've known each other for infinity. As though, even before infinity, the stars begged for us to be inseparable.

"Imagine me *not* being here," she says, silver bracelets dangling on her wrists as the hand that's not resting on my shoulder is holding onto a recyclable plate, her lips twitching in amusement.

“Things aren’t perfect,” I say for a few moments, watching as Laura’s gaze flickers over to me.

“Perfect is overrated,” she finally says, her shoulders brushing against mine in an easy nudge.

“Or maybe,” I begin, voice soft. “This is my version of perfect. *This*,” my hand waves over the area. Everyone who's here, my family, my friends. Everyone that I would fight hard for and everyone who would fight harder for me. “This is my perfect.”

Laura nods. A smirk curves onto her lips as she sets her plate down, hands finding her hips. “Try and make it to the other end before me?”

A laugh. “Try? You’re insanely slow.”

Her eyes flash with vibrance. “We’ll see.”

In seconds, Laura is running, her hair flickering behind her in a mess of black, and then I’m behind her, running like my life depends on it.

And I’m flying, laughing, screaming, and shouting out yells of euphoria into the cerulean sky.

I'm on top of clouds, harnessing the universe like it's always belonged to me.

Crying out, I will my feet to catch up to Laura as they fly over the clouds of grass and dirt, weaving around everyone that feels like blood to me.

The stars belong to us at this moment in time.

My chest swells.

And hell, I wouldn't have it any other way.

acknowledgements

I like to think of this book as something vital, something I've poured my life into. However, as with all accomplishments, this could have never been done without the assistance of those close to me.

Firstly, my parents with constant support from the sidelines and on the playing field. Secondly, many of the people around me, thoroughly scanning over this book and suggesting pieces of feedback.

All in all, many thanks go out to all those close to me, as you were crucial in helping me paint Amina Davis' world for her audience, and for that, I can't be more grateful.

www.ingramcontent.com/pod-product-compliance
Lightning Source LLC
Chambersburg PA
CBHW010403310726
48979CB00005B/1050
9781778098406